Rod spun around on his stool.

To his disbelief, the primary-yellow Beetle he'd encountered earlier that day had just parked in the last vacant slot outside the diner. Through the wide plate-glass window, he watched the woman step out of the car. Her long, Indian-cotton paisley skirt kept all its wrinkles and creases, even as it swirled around her ankles. A white tank top contrasted with her tanned shoulders. Heavy silver jewelry, by the looks of it handmade and expensive, gleamed against her dark honey skin. Straight black hair reached the middle of her back, and as she stared at the diner, Rod caught a glimpse of her feet.

He shook his head. "Look at that! She's even wearing Birkenstocks."

"Birka-whos?" Deely asked, her attention riveted on the new arrival.

"Birkenstocks," he repeated. "They're clunky leather and cork sandals from Germany. They're almost mandatory footwear for certain groups of. . .oh, let's say earthy people."

Deely's silver curls bobbed with her nod, but her gaze remained fixed on the foreigner. "German, you say?"

"Yes."

He could almost hear the gears in the elderly woman's brain crank around.

She met his gaze. "German car and German shoes. Wonder what she's doing here instead of there."

Josh gave another laugh. "She sure didn't come here to find peace and the summer of love—"

A sharp hiss sliced through the deputy's words. Girlish shrieks and boyish howls came from the kitchen. Loud whistles—metallic, not human—followed, and all culminated in a violent burst.

GINNY AIKEN, a former newspaper reporter, lives in Pennsylvania with her husband of twenty-eight years and their kids. She's the mother of four sons, one daughter-in-law, and two dogs...er, furred people. Born in Havana, Cuba, and raised in Venezuela, she wrote her first novel at age fifteen (and burned it a year later) while training with the Ballets de Caracas, later known as the Venezuelan National Ballet. An eclectic mix of jobs, of which her favorites remain wife, mother, and herder of her children's numerous and assorted friends, drove her to the computer and fiction in search of sanity. She is now the author of nineteen published works, but is still looking for that sanity.

Hunt for
Home

Ginny Aiken

Heartsong Presents

To my family: George; Ivan and Shiloh, Greg, Geoff, and Grant; plus Lisa and Cassie. Special thanks to John Burgan, Assistant Director and Tour Manager extraordinaire of the Crossmen Drum and Bugle Corps, for Blanche.

note from the Author:
I love to hear from my readers! You may correspond with me by writing:

Ginny Aiken
Author Relations
PO Box 719
Uhrichsville, OH 44683

ISBN 1-59310-544-4

HUNT FOR HOME

Our mission is to publish and distribute inspirational products offering exceptional value and biblical encouragement to the masses.

Scripture taken from the Holy Bible, New International Version®. NIV®. Copyright © 1973, 1978, 1984 by International Bible Society. Used by permission of Zondervan. All rights reserved.

PRINTED IN THE U.S.A.

one

Eden, Texas—present day

Had God plunked Adam and Eve down around this Eden instead of the other, the human race would never have made it.

After she'd driven for more hours than she cared to calculate on last night's two hours of uneasy sleep, Casey figured this stretch of road was deserted enough, therefore safe enough, for her to pull over and take a break, maybe even a nap. A great deal of deliberation went into that decision. A lot could be said for air conditioning in the Texas heat.

She didn't pull over right away. The air rushing in the windows of her vintage VW Bug felt better than it would if the car stood still. From the depths of the woven leather purse on the passenger seat, she withdrew her second to-last bottle of water and swigged down half its lukewarm contents in one gulp. Outside, she saw nothing but dun-colored sand bisected by the dark ribbon of road.

For the millionth time, a niggle of fear made her dig inside her bag for the map. She accordioned the cumbersome thing, found the fat dot of Dallas and the flyspeck of Eden, and connected the two via a spider web of unremarkable roadway.

Less than a minute later, she had to backhand the dampness from her forehead and yield to the inevitable. The relentless slap of hot air made her groan, but she still pulled the car over to the side of the road.

No breeze.

She didn't want to die like this, roasted to a crisp inside her little car out in the middle of the Texas desert. And no matter

5

which way she turned the clumsy map—upside down, right side up, or even catty-corner—she couldn't figure out where she was.

It figured.

Calamity Casey had struck again.

She grimaced and crumpled the map onto the seat at her side then leaned her head back. With eyes closed against the tears that threatened, she fought to keep snippets of old conversations from her mind.

And failed.

As usual.

"Are you *sure* you can handle this?" her father had asked just days ago, his thick, white brows drawn close over his straight nose. "You've never shown interest in cooking or the food industry, sweetheart, much less gained the experience needed to run a restaurant. This is no game."

She'd fought the flare of her temper, as well as her chronic fear of failure. "I know it's not, Dad. It's your business, the family's business, and I want to contribute. You said the Saylors have a staff in place. The way I see it, all I have to do is make sure everything continues to run smoothly while you and Mom find a buyer for their restaurant."

Her father slanted a sideways look at her.

"That's my point," he said. "The Garden of Eatin' must remain profitable if we're to serve the Saylors well. They chose Hunt Property Sales and Management to handle the sale of their business because they trust us. That trust is based on years of successful transactions, and I can't let them down."

Something inside Casey shrank. "I promise, Dad. I won't let you down—or your clients." She blinked away the tears and swallowed against the lump in her throat. "Please give me the chance."

The plea in her voice must have done the trick, because Dad had nodded then walked back to the oak file cabinet to pull a slender folder from the middle drawer. She'd tasted victory when he'd handed her a copy of the contract; keys to the diner and the Saylors' apartment; banking and insurance information; instructions and directions; and sent her on her way. And now she was lost in a world of sand.

Casey's eyelids drooped. She shook her head, rolled her shoulders, and considered a short walk. But the thought of a trudge through the heat made her tongue stick to the roof of her mouth. She had only one bottle of water left.

After she'd turned onto this stretch of road, she'd seen no other vehicle. According to the package the automobile club had put together for her, she had to be pretty close to Eden by now. But the lack of sleep and the nervous strain of the last few days had taken their toll.

She set her watch, with all its fancy buttons, bells, and doodads, to wake her in an hour. Then she let sleep have the upper hand.

No sooner had she dozed off, or so it seemed, than damp, musky hot air pumped over her face in rhythmic waves. Whether the odor, the mugginess, or the snuffles and thuds outside awoke her, Casey didn't know. All she knew when she opened her eyes was that she'd lost her mind, and she was about to be smothered by a bunch of big, fat, stinky cows.

The bovine's head pushed deeper into the car. Casey's heartbeat kicked into high gear. Panic set in.

"N—nice B—b—bossy. . ."

The beast's ear twitched, a major occurrence inside the close confines of the VW Bug.

Hysteria surged through her.

She reached for her bag with her right hand, her movements subtle and smooth, so as not to startle her hairy new companion. Did cellular service work out here?

Tears welled up, and she gulped. She should have listened to Dad. She wasn't prepared to deal with a bovine-filled life of insanity.

With shaky fingers, she dialed 911 and pressed the phone to her ear. When the dispatcher answered, a tsunami of words ripped from Casey's tongue.

"I *know* there are no cows in heaven"—the fear shoved her alto voice right up to a shrill falsetto—"so I'm not dead, and there's a cow in my car!"

"Excuse me?" the operator said.

Casey tried a deep breath but discovered that fetid cattle smells unsettled her stomach. "I thought I was dreaming, but I can't be, and I'm going to throw up if someone doesn't get this cow out of my car."

"Is this some kind of prank? Because if it is, ma'am, it's against the law, you know."

A sob hitched Casey's breath. "I wish it was a prank, but I'm really in trouble. Actually, I'm *in* my car, who-knows-where out here in the desert—but it is in Texas, unless I'm even more lost than I think I am—and I just woke up, and when I did, there was a cow in the window."

Dead silence met her idiotic explanation. Then, before she could do better, "What kind of car do you drive?"

"A Bug. From the sixties, not those new egg-shaped ones."

"Let's try this again," the emergency dispatcher said, false patience in her voice. "How much did you have to drink?"

Casey sputtered. "Nothing!"

Inches away, the cow's ear danced a jig, her nostrils flared, and her huge eye blinked.

Casey gasped then turned to her right, only to find her companion's twin eyeing them but not yet partaking in the invasion of the Bug.

She needed help, and for that she had to get the woman on the other end of the connection to take her seriously. Just what she'd tried to do her whole life with everyone she knew. Without success.

A deep breath didn't change a thing. She went on,

nonetheless. "Ma'am, I don't drink—not a drop. And I don't do drugs, unless you consider ibuprofen a drug, which I guess it is, but not in the way you mean, you know. And I'm really sane, just not the most successful person in the world, which is why I drive an ancient car. That and because I really like the vintage Bugs. . . ."

She shut up. Nerves always made her babble like an idiot—just when she needed to sound her most calm, cool, and collected.

"Could you describe these cows, ma'am?" the operator asked, a mixture of amusement and disbelief in her voice.

"Moooo!" answered Bossy. A powerful odor escaped her mouth.

"Please," Casey said on the verge of tears, "can you send someone to get these animals away from me? Then I'll leave, and I won't bother you again. I promise."

"One moment, ma'am." The phone clicked at the same time Casey heard what sounded like a drum roll in the distance. Her heart began to pound at that same rapid-fire rate. She wasn't about to be stampeded on top of everything else, was she?

Off to her right, somewhere in the middle of all that tan sand, a speedy cloud billowed forward. The noise grew louder. Actually, its cadence amplified at the same pace the cloud moved. It looked like help was on its way.

"Ma'am?" she said. "I think someone's discovered his missing cows, and he's coming for them now. I'm sorry I bothered you, but I won't need you anymore. Thank you so much for your—"

For what? Casey stared at the phone. What had the woman done for her?

Nothing.

Just as no one had ever done anything for her.

Well, that wasn't quite right. Her family had always bailed her out of trouble. And now it looked as though the Lone

Ranger had taken over the job. But was that real help? It struck her more like a search and rescue mission—after the fact, so to speak.

The realization killed Casey's nausea better than a whole bottle of pink stuff could have done. She folded her phone shut.

"Enough," she said.

The cow's head tilted a millimeter or so.

"You know, Bossy? I'm sick of this."

Bossy blinked.

"Yes, I am. And I'm done with the whole Calamity Casey deal, too."

Bossy's ear quivered.

Casey squared her shoulders—gingerly, of course. She didn't want to lock proverbial horns with Bossy.

"This is it," she told the mercifully placid animal. "You'll see. I'll prove to them I can do it. I'll do such a great job at the diner that they'll—they'll. . .well, I don't know what they'll do, but I'm going to do it anyway. I'm going to do it up right this time. You'll see."

The dust cloud parted and Casey got a look at the horse and rider. Nervous laughter burst forth. Lone Ranger? Not exactly.

This guy rode a huge black horse whose coat bore a sifting of sand. And while he could be nothing but a cowboy, the rider didn't look very heroic or mythic in the least. Instead, he looked like a dusty, hardworking Joe, dressed in well-faded jeans, plaid cotton shirt with sleeves folded up on his ropey forearms, a straw hat, and scuffed leather boots.

Horse and rider came closer, and Casey got a glimpse at the face shaded by the hat's brim. *Uh-oh.* He didn't look happy. Not one bit.

In a smooth, powerful motion he swung a leg over the horse's back and slid to the ground. He approached her, and only then did she hear a dog's yaps. It was busy nipping at

Bossy's and her pal's heels. Muffled by the animal's excited barks, she caught snippets of her rescuer's words.

"Common sense of a chicken. . .as if I didn't have enough to do. . . ."

Did he mean the cows or her? By the time he reached Bossy, Casey wasn't sure whether she wanted to thank him for coming after his cows or to give him an attitude adjustment—for free, without him even asking.

But when he got Bossy's head out of her window, Casey began to quiver. The effects of the adrenaline she'd expended during her little. . .adventure ran the gamut, and now she felt weak, weepy, and weary.

So she yelled her thanks over yapped and mooed complaints, then turned her map this way, that way, then this way one more time, and looked out the windshield. Nothing had changed. The road still ran dead ahead. If her directions were right, and she had no reason to question them just because she hadn't caught a glimpse of civilization for way too long, she would have to keep on heading down that way. Sooner or later, she hoped, she'd hit the town of Eden.

At least now Casey knew better than to expect paradise at the end of her trek.

two

"How's it going, boy?" called Whit Tucker. The elderly gent held court, as usual, in the rocking chair on his front porch. "What all's got you in such a snit? Don't reckon I see you look this cross-wires but oncet or twice a year."

Rod Harmon, Eden's chief of police, winced. "You're right, Whit. No point in letting something so silly as a lost tourist get under my skin."

The rocker's motion never faltered. "What happened?"

Rod dragged his hat off and wiped his forehead with a handkerchief. He then wasted no time in shielding his eyes again from the glare of the late spring sun.

"Couple of head from Mort Spencer's herd took off, and he called me to go after them—"

"That boy still laid up with that busted-up leg of his?"

That "boy" was fifty-three and a granddaddy to boot, but Rod figured that by Whit's count, anything under seventy was mere adolescence.

"Sure is, and he'd sent his hired hands out to brand calves this morning."

Whit's faded blue eyes narrowed. "And he knew you wouldn't a said no."

"It's my job to help out—"

"It sure ain't your job to go after a fool rancher's cattle whenever it ain't handy for 'im to do so hisself, *Chief*."

"It was early, and I knew Josh would be in the office in time." He'd had this discussion with the elderly gent so many times they both might as well have read it off a script. "Besides, I don't have it in me to turn someone down if I can

12

help. You know that."

"I just know that's why you're dragging, boy. Ya ain't gonna do this town any good if you wear yourself out, you know. You gotta rest, have yourself some fun ever oncet in a while." A scratch to his head left the sparse hairs askew. "Say, when's the last time you had a date?"

Even Rod couldn't remember. "I'm fine, Whit. Don't you worry, now."

With a tap to his hat brim, Rod walked on, his sights set on lunch. For him, breakfast, lunch, and dinner meant he'd pop in and settle down to one of Shirley and Herb Saylor's meals. Not for the calorie counters, the food the couple prepared and served their friends and neighbors came loaded with fat, salt, sugar, and love.

Rod savored every last, delicious crumb.

But now the Saylors had decided to sell. He didn't begrudge them their retirement, not with Herb's ticker in such bad shape, but he sure was going to miss them. He heartily hoped that whoever bought the Garden of Eatin' didn't change a thing about the place.

The diner was the heart and soul of Eden, Texas.

Icy air greeted him when he pushed open the door. Greetings rang out from booths against the walls and the stools along the counter. He doffed his hat and smiled, then nodded and shook hands as he went to his usual spot on the stool by the corner window—right across from the pie case.

Rotund Deely Billings popped up at his elbow just as his behind touched down. "Saw you ride out on that big, black monster horse of yours." Her gray eyes danced in a face lined with decades of life under the hard Texas sun. "Care to share who you went huntin'?"

"Sorry to disappoint, but it was only a pair of Mort's cows that got loose today. Had to go get them back for him."

Disappointment made the mass of wrinkles sag. "Oh."

Sympathy for the lonely spinster dredged up the memory of the woman Rod found while on his roundup mission.

"You know?" he said. "I did have an interesting encounter while I was at it."

Deely took her time climbing onto the empty stool at his side. He would have picked up the plump lady and perched her on the seat, but he knew better. It'd take him months to recover from the tongue-lashing she would mete out.

"Well?" she said, her feet a full three inches above the steel footrest. "You going to make an old woman beg?"

He chuckled. "Not hardly, Cordelia Billings. Just let me order me some lunch, and I'll give you all the details."

Sarah Anne Woods answered his wave. "Hey there, Chief Rod. What can I get for you today?"

"What's the special?"

The girl frowned then shrugged. "I'm not rightly sure, sir. Mr. and Mrs. Saylor left in a rush last night to catch that surprise cruise their kids gave them."

Rod glanced through the opening in the wall behind the counter. He saw no one at the grill. "So who's cooking? Who's in charge?"

A blush tinted her cheekbones. "Sam Brueger volunteered to keep an eye on things. He's *so* helpful and talented and strong and smart—"

"We get the picture," he said to stem Sarah Anne's paeans of the kid. "I didn't know he could cook."

She giggled. "He didn't either. But don't worry. Me an' Mandy an' Will an' Stu are helping him. I'm sure everything'll be awesome. *He's* awesome."

Deely tittered. He glanced her way and saw her roll her eyes. Unease filled his otherwise empty stomach.

"See if you can rustle up some meat loaf and mashed potatoes for me, would you, please?"

"Yes, sir."

When she didn't go give his order to the awesome Sam, but rather stayed at his side and shifted from foot to foot, Rod looked her straight in the eye. "Okay. So what's up this time?"

"Well, nothing, sir. I just wondered who was going to play for Sunday's service now Mrs. Saylor's gone. No one else knows how to run that big old organ up to the church."

His unease grew. "You know, Sarah Anne, I've given this up to the Lord. So far, all I know is that I'll bring my guitar with me. I'm sure the Father has a plan for us."

Rod had prayed and prayed for God to reveal that plan. As the part-time music minister at Eden's Church of the Rock, he had to find someone to accompany the congregation's worship, but so far, he'd had no success. The older folks in their midst would only see his strumming as an unorthodox temporary fix.

"You could let Sam and Nikki and Trevor play with you, you know," Sarah Anne offered.

Deely gasped. Her fluffy white eyebrows flew up to her spiked lavender hair.

"Tell you what, Sarah Anne," Rod said, "I have to hurry back to my other job, so why don't you take my food order to the kitchen and see about feeding this hungry chief of police?"

The teenager blushed again and scurried off, her perky brown ponytail bouncing with her every step.

"Tell me you won't let them crazy kids break our eardrums with their caterwauling and drumming and amplifiers and all that," Deely demanded, her jaw out more than an inch.

"Only as a last resort."

"Phew!" She relaxed then pinned him with her stare. "Well? What about that encounter of yours?"

He'd all but forgotten his morning's experience. "It was the craziest thing. I went after those two cows and found one of them with her head stuck in the window of an old Beetle."

"A what?"

"You know, those little Volkswagen cars that are round"—
he drew an approximation in the air—"the ones Mom and
Dad told me they used to pile bunches of kids inside just
to see how many they could fit. Seems Mort's cows had the
same idea."

"Yeah. The hippies used to love them."

"Evidently they still do."

"Huh?"

"The woman inside this one looked like she made a wrong
turn back in San Francisco's 1969."

"No!"

"Yes, ma'am."

"You don't say. So. You're saying we better watch out.
Them hippies are coming."

Josh Adams, Eden's lone patrolman, laughed. "Looks more
like they're already here."

Deely stiffened.

Rod spun around on his stool.

To his disbelief, the primary-yellow Beetle he'd encountered
earlier that day had just parked in the last vacant slot outside
the diner. Through the wide plate-glass window, he watched
the woman step out of the car. Her long, Indian-cotton paisley
skirt kept all its wrinkles and creases, even as it swirled around
her ankles. A white tank top contrasted with her tanned
shoulders. Heavy silver jewelry, by the looks of it handmade
and expensive, gleamed against her dark honey skin. Straight
black hair reached the middle of her back, and as she stared at
the diner, Rod caught a glimpse of her feet.

He shook his head. "Look at that! She's even wearing
Birkenstocks."

"Birka-whos?" Deely asked, her attention riveted on the
new arrival.

"Birkenstocks," he repeated. "They're clunky leather and cork sandals from Germany. They're almost mandatory footwear for certain groups of. . .oh, let's say earthy people."

Deely's silver curls bobbed with her nod, but her gaze remained fixed on the foreigner. "German, you say?"

"Yes."

He could almost hear the gears in the elderly woman's brain crank around.

She met his gaze. "German car and German shoes. Wonder what she's doing here instead of there."

Josh gave another laugh. "She sure didn't come here to find peace and the summer of love—"

A sharp hiss sliced through the officer's words. Girlish shrieks and boyish howls came from the kitchen. Loud whistles—metallic, not human—followed, and all culminated in a violent burst.

Four members of the Church of the Rock's youth group ran out. Each wrestled his or her apron ties and hurried toward the door.

Sarah Anne, pale under her freckles, her brown eyes wider than Rod had ever seen them, shot him a frightened look. "I—I quit!"

Sam, the "awesome" one, tried to preserve his dignity, but beneath his tan his skin revealed a gray cast. "I just remembered. Coach wants to hold linebacker practice today at"—he glanced at the clock above the door—"exactly two o'clock. Can't be late—only got two hours. Gotta go!"

He tried to swagger but the baggy pants that hung a good three inches below his waist and the fear he couldn't quite mask hampered his efforts. He hitched up the denim and beat a hasty retreat.

Mandy Judge cried, "Wait for me!"

Rich Norman threw his immaculate apron on the counter. "I'm outta here."

All four ran down the street.

Bubbling noises came from the kitchen, and a couple of customers sent worried looks in that direction. Since no one seemed eager to investigate the cause, Rod figured he'd better see what kind of danger threatened the diner and its customers.

As he rounded the counter, Josh called out. "Hey, Rod. See if those kids got my burger ready while you're in there. I can't take much longer for lunch."

"Yeah," Chucky Moore chimed in. At close to six foot six and three hundred pounds, no sane person came between the postal employee and his food. "I'd a chicken-fried steak dinner platter with a side of cheeseburger and fries coming. And I'm hungry."

Someone called for her grilled cheese and pickles, while a chorus of "Coffee!" and "Pie!" bounced off the walls.

Rod's nerves stretched guitar-string tight, but he kept a smile on his face. He stepped forward and cast a last look over his shoulder at the ravenous horde. "Let me see what I can do."

As the customers groused behind him, Rod faced the kitchen. What he found gave a grown man cause to cry, but as the town's chief of police, he didn't have the luxury.

He had to keep the peace in the diner, but he didn't have a clue how. Even cooking for himself was out of his jurisdiction. And now this.

The massive coffee machine that kept the Garden of Eatin' in business gave off forlorn burps and moans while spurts of steam spewed ceilingward. A trickle of mud-colored water dripped from one of the spigots that normally served up rivers of Shirley Saylor's excellent blend of java, and hot, wet coffee grounds clung to every surface nearby.

He'd known that morning, when he picked up the phone at thirteen minutes past four, that today was going to be one of the rough ones. A man in his position, one he'd held for the last four years, came to learn these things mighty quick.

He just hadn't realized then how rough it would get.

❧

No wonder the owners of the Garden of Eatin' had decided to sell. Casey turned to evaluate the undeniable main drag of Eden, Texas, and groaned. She'd sell, too. This was no paradise.

A trickle of sweat rolled down the middle of her back, and she picked up the heavy length of her hair to give her neck a reprieve.

Why, oh, why hadn't she listened to her dad? But no. She'd just had to beg to be sent into this hot cauldron of a town—all because she was desperate to prove herself as more than the family mess-up.

She was tired of pats on the head. She couldn't stomach one more patronizing look. And she hoped and prayed she'd never have to hear one more "It's just Casey's lot in life."

If she had anything to say about it, failure in Eden, Texas, was *not* going to be her lot in life. She meant to keep things on an even keel, man the helm at the diner, and show each and every last one of her relatives that she could run a shipshape operation.

Then. . .

She shrugged. She'd worry about "then" once she got there. No sense biting off any more than she could chew.

She shook her head. *Yeah, right.* She'd already done that, by the looks of things.

A deep breath and a straightened spine gave her the resolve to face the Garden of Eatin'—with an apostrophe in purple neon, no less—again. But as she did, she heard a commotion inside the diner.

Mere moments later, the door flew open and four teenagers pelted out. Their faces bore panic and horror, and Casey had a feeling that things were already far from shipshape inside.

"It would be just my luck," she muttered. She reached through the Bug's open window and picked up her purse. The voice of one of the girls, now running down the street as fast as her legs could go, wafted back to her.

"I told you it was gonna blow!"

The other one answered—faintly, "I'm not waiting another table there."

Sick dread sank into her middle. "Alrighty then, here I go. Can't make it any worse than that, now, can I?"

As she sailed into the icy restaurant, Casey noted the unhappy faces turned her way. A second ago, they'd all stared out the window, more curious than anything else. Or so she'd thought.

Now? She hadn't even had a chance to wreak havoc, and they already appeared mad at her. But they couldn't be. Not yet.

Could their displeasure have something to do with whatever the teen had predicted would blow?

The strong aroma of coffee caught her attention. Too bad the stuff didn't taste half as good as it smelled. She could use something to brace herself right then, something that might give her the energy and, to be honest, the courage she lacked.

If she'd learned only one thing from her calamitous misadventures, it was to hold her head high and go on. And so she did.

Casey approached the counter with all the aplomb she could muster. "I'd like to speak to either Mr. or Mrs. Saylor."

At the far right end of the counter, a little old lady with spiked purple hair cackled a dry laugh.

"You'll have to hurry to the Med-it-terranean to do it," she said, her Texas twang cut only by the rare, precise diction. "They left yesterday for their cruise."

Casey's already unsteady stomach, thanks to her encounter

with Bossy and friend on the highway, lurched at her growing dismay. "But. . .I didn't get here yesterday. I'm here now."

The huge man in the postal uniform arched his brow. "And that's supposed to mean. . . ?"

"How could they leave without me? I mean, I didn't get here yesterday. How do they expect me to take over for them if they don't even show me what it is they do?"

"Care to tell us who you are?"

The deep voice came from the direction of what Casey assumed was the door to the kitchen. She turned and felt her stomach sink right down to her toes.

She knew the guy. She'd seen him before. And not when she'd been at her best. It was just her luck that her Lone Ranger/average Joe would wind up at the Garden of Eatin'. And was he ever a hunk! A frowning hunk.

"Uh. . . I'm Casey Hunt."

He stepped toward her, questions evident in his blue eyes. "Welcome to Eden, Casey Hunt. How may I help you?"

"Oh, no. You can't help me. I'm here to help you." *That wasn't right.* "I mean I'm here to help Mr. and Mrs. Saylor. With the diner, you see. I'm Bob and Wendy Hunt's daughter."

"I'm sure they're real proud, " he said, a twinkle in his eyes. "But how do you intend to help folks who've left? And what's that got to do with your family tree?"

Was there a giant mirror somewhere in this place? Was her name really Alice rather than Casey, and had she just walked right through into Wonderland? Maybe it was more like la–la land.

"Let me explain." *Lord, please help me here, because I'm just as confused.* "The Saylors signed a contract with Hunt Property Sales and Management—HPSM—so they would put the diner up for sale. My father is Robert Hunt, the owner of HPSM. The Saylors also contracted for a temporary manager—while they're not here and the place is up for sale. I'm it."

The hunk's smile twitched, and Casey suspected he was fighting a laugh. Why did these things keep happening to her? What was so funny?

She blew out an exasperated breath, but before she could speak, he said, "It?"

Casey nodded.

He persisted. "It what?"

"It. The manager."

The twitch grew stronger, and she saw him struggle to keep his composure. But when the little old lady in the corner began to cackle, followed by the man in the business suit and the huge mountain of a postal worker wedged into the nearest booth, the hunk lost the battle.

He laughed.

No, laughter was too subtle a term for what he did. He howled, he guffawed, and the rest of the customers followed suit.

That is, they did until a loud *whoosh* in the kitchen caught everyone's attention. Sharp crackles followed, and a rosy glow backlit the cowboy in the doorway. The smell of barbecue grill hit Casey's nose at the same time a teenaged boy shoved said cowboy from behind.

"I'm outta here," the kid yelled on his way out the door. "I don't care how much I promised the Saylors I'd stay on the job. Someone else's gonna have to cook."

Casey froze. She met the good-looking guy's blue gaze. She gasped.

She then fisted her hands, closed her eyes, and yelled, *"Fire!"*

three

Casey gulped in a lungful of air, but she'd held her breath for so long that she had to inhale again and yet again before she convinced her lungs they would survive. As she continued to fight for breath and avoid hyperventilating—for which she had an unfortunate knack—the cowboy went into rescue mode for the second time that day.

He yanked the red fire extinguisher from its perch on the wall and aimed its funneled hose at the massive, flaming grill and the grease that had spilled onto the floor.

Casey, breathe! Her brain's command trickled down to her lungs, and she gasped for air.

She recoiled at the sudden, loud noise coming from the fire extinguisher. A cloud of foam billowed from it and blanketed the grill and spattered grease. A tap on her shoulder made her turn. The little old lady whose day she'd made earlier bounced from side to side, curiosity in her eyes, determined to miss none of the action.

Casey gave her a generous slice of doorway, but she'd already missed seeing Eden's Lone Ranger do his thing.

He was good.

Now he stood and surveyed the devastation, extinguisher still at the ready, legs spread, gaze on the stove, his expression dismayed.

She could see why—anyone could. Black soot covered the wall behind the monster stove and reached even the ceiling above. Clumps of gloppy grease made the floor a minefield. And whatever the kid who'd just quit had tried to cook now looked like lumps of foam-frosted charcoal.

The customers would not be happy.

"Whoo-ee!" the old woman said, her voice full of awe. "Galloping gizzards."

Although Casey had no clue what a galloping gizzard might be, she did identify with the lady's wonderment—horror, really. "Someone's got quite the mess to clean up."

Her elderly companion shot her a glance. "Someone?" she asked. "You just told us all you're the manager now. Seems to me *you've* got yourself a mess of cleaning to do."

Casey gaped then clamped her jaw shut. She scrabbled through her now useless brain for words but found none. She tried to speak, but only a squawk came out. Again she closed her mouth and worked to keep the tears unshed.

From the booth closest to the door, the giant mailman called out. "Hey, lady. Since you're the manager, manage me my lunch, will ya? I gotta get back to work, but I won't be worth a lick if I don't eat."

Casey spun. His broad face hadn't seen a shaver in a couple of days, and she wondered if he'd tried to make a fashion statement or he'd just chosen not to bother. Either way, his bulk and the five-o'clock shadow gave him an intimidating air.

She squared her shoulders. She should try to see if his food had survived the blaze. "What did you order?"

A smile curved the thicket of stubble. "A chicken-fried steak dinner platter with a side of burger and fries—no mayo on that. Gotta watch my cholesterol, ya know."

Casey gawked. "You're kidding!"

"No, ma'am," the giant said. A frown replaced the smile. "I want my food, and I want it now." He scoffed. "I sure wish Herb and Shirley hadn't gone on that cruise."

A rustle of yeses swept the room. Casey couldn't believe she'd already landed in such hot water. She'd only been in Eden and at the Garden of Eatin' for less than—she glanced at her watch—unbelievable! The longest nine minutes in history! Was that all?

"I'll check on the status of your order," she said in her most authoritative voice.

She walked into the kitchen and stopped short. Never in her twenty-five years had she seen the likes of it. Spilled food and utensils littered everything. "Wow."

"You don't say."

She looked at the cowboy, none too happy with his sarcasm. But instead of angry or accusatory, he, too, looked shell-shocked and dismayed.

"That man out there," she said, "the mailman. He wants his food."

Cowboy Hunk grinned. "That's Chucky for you. He has his priorities straight." He shoved the fire extinguisher back onto the metal holder on the wall and then looked over the handful of offerings on the steel counters. "Can't say I see anything that looks like chicken-fried steak, now, do you?"

Casey approached. She checked out the contents of the filled plates, but she saw nothing she could identify as Chucky's meal. She did see some strange lumps of pale yellow stuff, and if she stretched her imagination, she might manage to label them omelets gone wrong. An enormous bowl of some mayonnaise-based goop looked like it could be either chicken salad or tuna, but the dressing had been added with such a liberal hand that Casey could only guess at its original contents.

A sandwich made with burnt toast, wilted lettuce, and who-knew-what in the middle seemed ready to serve. It even had a handful of chips and two slices of pickle on the side. Casey doubted anyone would want a bite of the charred bread.

"Could the chicken-fried steak still be on the grill?" she asked.

Cowboy Hunk peered at the cooking surface. "Could be.

But if it is, then Chucky's out of luck."

She looked over her shoulder, and Chucky's expression gave her pause. "Hmm. . .since you put out the fire," she ventured, her nervous stomach tight and jumpy, "do you think. . .I mean, could you please. . .well, since you know him and I don't, would you please tell Chucky—*Mr.* Chucky— that his steak is dead?"

That twitchy smile he'd sported earlier returned. His blue eyes met hers, and Casey knew he'd seen what she'd tried to hide: He now knew she was chicken, if not the purveyor of a certain chicken-fried steak.

She blushed. "Please?"

"Tell you what." He reached for and grabbed a utilitarian white towel then tossed it at her. "See what you can swab up with this while I give Chucky the news."

She caught the cloth but couldn't pick a logical place to start, so she followed to see how the customer would react.

Casey could have predicted Chucky's response. His eyes narrowed, his brow furrowed, his jaw worked, and his lips pursed. Finally, and with great effort, he wriggled out from behind the table, stood to his phenomenal height, and threw down his paper napkin in obvious disgust.

"Tell you what, Chief," he said on his way to the door. "This sure ain't the way to keep folks from moving away from Eden. Fix this, or you're plain spinning your wheels on all the rest."

Chief? The handsome cowboy was a chief? What kind of chief? His hair was too blond for a tribal leader, so that left her two choices. Either he was the chief of the local fire department, which his handy-work with the extinguisher suggested he might be, or else he was the chief of police. The way her luck was running, this was the town's top cop. In either case, she was in trouble.

Casey wished the floor would open under her feet, but of all the calamities that had already beset her this day, that refused to become one of them.

"It's just a little pothole in our road map," the lawman said. Casey noted his stiffened shoulders.

He went on. "The Garden of Eatin' has a new manager, now. Remember, Chuck?"

In the kitchen doorway, Casey felt the weight of myriad stares. To add to the off-kilter sensation—not to mention the panic she tried to suppress—she felt tension spark to life among the customers in the diner. Something was up here in Eden, and she feared she'd just stepped right in it. It stunk.

At the door, Chucky paused to glare back at her. "If she can boil an egg a body can eat, I'll—well, I'll eat my hat."

"Why not the egg?" Casey asked before she could bite her tongue.

Someone laughed. Chucky shook his head and left. Casey wished she might vanish into thin air. As she twisted her fingers and tried to think of a way to fix this mess, a clicking approached from the door. A moment later, she spotted the source.

"Oh, no!" The biggest, hairiest, ugliest mutt she'd ever seen shambled toward her. Its long, matted brown coat looked like it hadn't been on the right side of a brush, soap, or water in months, maybe years. Through its shaggy thatch of brow, a pair of woebegone brown eyes pled for pity, and a black button nose shone out from within the bristle of hair on the muzzle.

"Out!" she cried. "This is a restaurant. No shoes, no shirt, no service."

The laughter spread.

She persisted. "Go! You're unsanitary. You can't stay."

"Well, missy, why don't you lead him out if you don't want him?" asked a middle-aged woman in a plain blue blouse and skirt. She patted the creature's head on her way to the door.

Why did this have to be her day for beasts? "Well, because. . . because. . .hey! He's bigger than I am!"

A woman and two little girls, all three redheads wearing matching pink shorts and tops, the mom in a ponytail and her preschoolers in pigtails, followed the more severe woman, their chuckles not the support Casey hoped for. They didn't pet the dog, but the girls looked like they wanted to. She shuddered.

"Waitress!"

Casey looked around but saw no one serving tables. Then she realized the suited man had his gaze on her.

"Me?" Great. Now she sounded like a squeak toy.

"Of course, you," he said before she could utter another word. "You said you were the manager, so I reckon you're in charge now. I need another cup of coffee."

The panic won the war. She looked from side to side, turned, took a step toward the kitchen, backed up again. Had she seen coffee anywhere? Besides those grounds glopped all over the kitchen, that is. "Uh. . ."

"Here ya go." The cop shoved a pot at her.

She dropped the towel she'd clutched like a security blanket and grabbed the brown plastic handle instead. On shaky legs, she approached the customer and, with the utmost care, filled his ceramic mug. To her relief, she noted his crumb-dusted plate. At least he'd been fed.

He looked up. "Cream?"

Casey gulped. "Uh, I'll see what I can do."

She ran to the kitchen, shot looks at the stove, the counters, the sinks—were they ever *big*—the huffing and puffing coffee machine. Where was the fridge?

As she tried to identify that appliance in the endless expanse of steel, the clicking announced the dog's arrival. "No! Not in the kitchen. You shed, you drool, you—you probably have fleas and ticks."

Then the canine invader led her right to the cream. His bright pink tongue slurped up the thick, white pool on the floor, the coffee grounds sprinkled on it no deterrent to his enjoyment. Inches away, the half-gallon container lay on its side, a rivulet still seeping from the spout.

How could she go out there and tell the gentleman the dog had drunk his cream?

This time, Casey was powerless against the tears. She stayed where she was, in the center of the kitchen, helpless, hopeless, and disheartened. The fat teardrops rolled down her cheeks, silent and sincere.

Through a veil of misery, she saw the cop pick up two of the plates with food and head back out to the customers. His help only served to make her feel worse. It brought home all her failings.

She couldn't believe she'd already blown it, this time before she'd even done anything. *Dear God, why can't I do a single thing right?*

The dog's wet nose nudged her left hand. He seemed intent on gaining her acceptance. That oh-so-innocent look made something shift inside her. But she wasn't about to give in or give up. Not yet.

"Come on, you behemoth, you. You can't stay." She reached for a collar, but wads of fur hampered her search. Casey gathered the folds of her skirt and crouched low. "Let's see. There's got to be something in here."

The dogs she knew all had collars, tags—even microchips, some of them. This beast had to have some means by which to identify its neglectful owner.

She dug into the matted coat, her fingers gentle. But no matter how thorough her search, she found no means of identification. She also found nothing to hold on to and haul him away.

She stood and dusted off her hands. "Okay, big guy. We're going to get you out of here one way or another."

The dog cocked his head, and if she didn't know better she'd say he'd understood. She patted him between the ears.

"Yuck! You poor thing. Whoever's been taking care of you hasn't done a very good job. You're a mess."

She stepped around to his rear and, with as much dignity as she could muster, she planted her palms on his rump. She shoved.

He didn't budge.

"Help me out here, will you?" she asked the dog, pushing with all her might. "One thing, okay? I have to get one thing right today. Please be it."

She leaned her shoulder into the effort and slid the critter one millimeter over the gray linoleum floor. He grunted his displeasure.

"Too bad, buster. You may be bigger than me, ornerier than me, even stronger than me. But I'm in charge now, and you're out. Get a move on, Goliath. It's time for this David to win herself a battle."

Casey pushed.

She shoved.

She pressed her back up against that of the dog. She used every ounce of strength she possessed. The animal refused to help, but little by little Casey inched him toward the kitchen's back door and closer to victory.

"What are you doing?" the cop asked.

Goliath leaped aside.

Casey fell.

Spread-eagled flat on her back, she stared up at the ceiling. Coffee grounds splotched even that. She was going to have to ask about the deal with the java. But first she would have to stand up, and for that, she had to find a pinch of dignity, if not a bushel of grace.

As she prayed for help, the cop blocked her view of the ceiling. He looked gigantic from the floor, tall and tanned and trim, but the bewilderment on his chiseled features made her feel like a joke.

"Do you have any idea what you're up to, Moonbeam-Sunshine? Or is it Starflower, perhaps?"

Casey glared. "How dare you make fun of me!"

He shrugged, and his lips twitched as an eyebrow arched. "Those names just kind of seem right, for some reason."

"Well, you're way off, I'll have you know. My name's Casey Hunt—didn't I tell you that a little while ago?"

"Mmm. . ."

That little murmur told her nothing, but the muscular arms crossed over his chest said it all.

She rose up onto her elbows. "Anyway, my name's Casey Hunt, and that's more than you've shared. All I know about you is that they say you're the chief of police around here, but all I've seen is the biggest busybody I ever laid eyes on."

"I'm only trying to help."

She sat up. "Tell you what. I appreciate your help, but you can go back to—to whatever a chief of police does. I'll take care of things from here on in."

His mouth curved and the twitching increased. "*You're* going to take care of things? Everything? All by yourself?"

"Are you doubting my competence?" It never hurt to call on one's bravado when facing a rotten situation.

The cop raised his hands in defense. "Hey, far be it from me to cast aspersions on a stranger."

Casey narrowed her eyes. She hated mockery, especially when aimed her way. "That's a mighty big word for a cowboy to use. Maybe you ought to go take a rest, since it must have taken such a great deal of effort to come up with it."

His jaw muscles worked and anger gave his eyes a brittle glare. It seemed she'd struck a nerve with her barb, but he'd been pretty nasty himself. He'd thrown out the first, after all.

"Honest," she said, "you can go back to your—"

He closed his eyes and turned his face ceilingward. "I don't know why you chose to fling an insult at me," he said, his voice even with forced control, "even though I did tease you. I apologize for that, and I want you to know all I want is to help you get on your feet around here—no pun intended. It's pretty clear the place is a mess right now."

His apology appeared to cost him, and Casey wondered what had made him offer it. Regardless, he was right, which left her no alternative. "I'm sorry, too. I played on a stereotype to strike back at you, and that's wrong. I don't know you— not even your name."

He reached out his hand. "I'm Rod Harmon, Chief of Police of Eden, Texas. I figure I've been less than welcoming, too. Sorry about that."

She took hold of his warm, somewhat rough fingers and scrambled up onto her knees. "Well, you did try to help. And you got some meals out to the customers. But, really, I'm fine now. I can take over."

Casey didn't know why it mattered so much to get him out of the diner, but it did. And the sooner he left, the better she'd feel.

She gathered her voluminous skirt so as not to trip on her way up. "Thanks for the help. With the cows and with the customers out front."

"Anytime." He stepped toward the front of the diner then cast her a look over his shoulder. "I sure hope you know what you're doing, Casey, because from where I stand, all I can see is calamity on the diner's horizon."

Casey gasped. She lost her balance and fell back on her rump. She stared at Rod Harmon as he left the kitchen without another word.

He didn't need another one. He'd said enough.

More than enough.

How had he known? Did she have it stamped across her forehead or did it dangle from her neck?

Would she ever amount to more than Calamity Casey?

four

In the wake of Chief Rod Harmon's departure, Casey rose to her feet and stood frozen in place. She again fought tears.

She had to face facts. These things didn't just happen to her. She often chased ideas, leaped into situations for which she was anything but prepared. Then, when she tried to put her latest plan into action, she faced yet another defeat.

She was a calamity looking for a place to happen.

Eden, Texas, looked like the newest place.

Why couldn't she find that something she could be good at? Something at which she might excel? Something where her natural shyness didn't make her awkward, which always made her even more inept? Something where her efforts would pay off with success?

She wasn't stupid; she'd finished college. True, it took her six years instead of the usual four, but not because she lacked brains. She'd aced all her classes—all but the remedial pre-algebra they made her take to satisfy the ridiculous math requirement.

The experience still rankled. She took the course during summer school, hoping for one-on-one help since no one else had registered for the course. Things didn't work out quite like she'd planned.

She proved so inept at math that the professor had no recourse but to tutor her after class. But in spite of all her efforts, she failed miserably every quiz and test she took. After a long meeting, the dazed math department granted her a C for effort but also begged her to please not return.

Casey sniffed. As if she would have wanted to.

She soon dropped out of the elementary ed program and transferred to her third college. Those transfers almost did her in. Each school had its own esoteric criteria for what qualified a student for a degree. Casey always wound up on the wrong side of the credit count.

But that was in the past. Last spring, she donned cap and gown and received her diploma. She now held a bachelor of arts in humanities. Which prepared her for a career in nothing, really—a factor that played a huge role in her current predicament.

Since graduation, Casey had held six different jobs, each one a greater disaster than the one before.

She'd learned she wasn't cut out to sell insurance; she did no better as a bank teller—that math thing again, the rounding up and rounding down. Who knew a couple of pennies here and there would be such a big deal?

She then failed—spectacularly—as the administrative assistant to a high school principal, and her stints in human resources, marketing, and even cosmetics sales at the high-end mall store had reaped no better results.

Her shyness did her in each time.

So, without income, she'd had to move out of her cute apartment and back home with Mom and Dad. Then the Saylors decided to sell. The Hunts' family business was in its peak season and all of Dad's management teams were on assignment. They had no one to run the Garden of Eatin'. Surely, Casey had thought, she could tell people to keep up the good work they'd always done.

Hah!

She looked around the scorched kitchen—the *empty* scorched kitchen. Who was she going to tell to do what they'd always done? Who knew that Casey's propensity for disaster could and would precede her?

Could someone fail even before they arrived on the scene?

She'd so wanted to prove to Mom and Dad—the wildly successful Realtors—and her siblings—Rachel, the doctor of entomology; Doug, the pastor of one of Seattle's largest congregations; and Suzanne, the CEO of a cutting-edge cosmeceuticals manufacturer—that the baby of the family wasn't a mess after all.

She took a deep breath. They all shared the same gene pool. And she'd never heard of a mess-up gene in any of her varied and sundry courses. So why couldn't she succeed?

"Lord? If You're not too busy. . ." Casey preferred to believe He wasn't, even though she hadn't seen much evidence of His help in her life, and none of late. "I could really use a hand here. Would You help me out? Please don't let me fail again. *Please?*"

Although she didn't feel any different than before her prayer, Casey knew she couldn't just stand in a corner of the kitchen and wish and hope and pray. There were customers out there, and she had to serve them—they didn't call it customer service for nothing.

The glass coffeepot sat on the steel counter right by the door. "Everyone loves coffee," she murmured. "Except me, of course, but that doesn't matter right now." ·

Pot in hand, she sallied forth, a smile pasted on her face. She hoped it masked her nervousness.

"Who'd like some more coffee?"

Only two people remained in the place: the curious old lady who'd laughed at Casey, and another woman, this one in her early thirties and with her nose in a mystery novel.

Great. She'd barely landed, and she'd already cleared out the place.

Had the tiny, lavender-haired fan of mayhem already placed an order? And for what? What if she'd already paid and hadn't been served? How did the cash register operate?

Casey's heart sank. She hadn't a clue where to begin, she

had no staff to supervise, and the owners had left town, apparently without telling anyone they had someone coming to take over for them. What were they thinking?

But, no. She wouldn't—couldn't—let anything get her down again. She tamped down the urge to run and hide and approached the woman with the book. "Coffee?"

She looked up at Casey with gentle brown eyes. "Actually, I'd like my vegetable soup and grilled-chicken salad. Sarah Anne ran out of here so fast, I didn't get a chance to ask about them. Mine wasn't one of the meals Chief Rod served."

"It's under control, thanks. I'll see if I can find your order." Casey wiggled the half-full coffeepot. "Do you want some?"

The customer pointed at a glass wet with condensation. "I prefer ice water. I'm Marcia Cambridge, but please call me Marcie. I'm the principal at the high school—it's my first day of freedom this summer. What with all the excitement, I don't think anyone welcomed you to town, so I'd like to do it. If there's anything you need, please let me know. I'd be happy to help you settle in."

The warmth woven through Marcie's words seeped into Casey's heart. "Thank you. You're very kind. I'll keep that in mind."

Now she really had to find that soup and salad. She couldn't bear to send that nice woman away without her meal.

A quick look around found no soup and salad, but next to the enormous sink, Casey did see a couple of white cotton towels bunched together. Maybe. "Please, God, let there be soup and salad under there."

Relief flooded her when her prayer was answered. The towels had indeed covered the missing meal, but the food didn't inspire any confidence. The greens had wilted, the chicken—at least, the beige blobs looked more like chicken than anything else—struck her as tough and unattractive, and the cotton fabric had absorbed a good portion of the broth in the bowl. A few sad carrot coins, peas, celery slices, tomato bits, a soggy green leaf or two, and a handful of kernels of corn waded in the dregs of pale rose liquid.

She sighed. "Lord, I know I wasn't very specific, and I don't mean to tell You what to do, but do You think that when You answer another of my prayers You could give me just a teeny-weeny, little bit more in Your answer? I was hoping to serve Marcie something edible."

Casey grabbed the cold dishes and hurried to Marcie's side. But before she reached her new acquaintance, her shins met solid resistance, and she went flying. So did the salad and soup.

A great deal of sputtering followed her graceless fall. "Wouldja just look at that, you fool girl?" the old woman exclaimed. "You're so clumsy, you just went and cost me my whole seven bucks!"

Seven dollars? What had she done—besides fall and drop the principal's lunch? With great trepidation, Casey opened one hesitant eye. She groaned.

Bedecked in produce, the lady's cheeks had turned an admirable shade of puce. It didn't go well with her lavender hair, not even with the veggies that clung to various perches on her body and head.

"I'll have you know," the affronted elder continued, "that you've ruined Laverne's latest creation. And I'm none too happy. I didn't spend half my day at the Do or Dye—or pay good money—to wind up looking more like a Cabbage Patch Kid than a classy woman of the world."

Surprisingly spry, the lady scurried to the door and stormed away, her mutters unabated.

Tears flooded Casey's eyes.

A thick, wet something swabbed her face. Only then did she notice the dog that had cushioned her fall. The mammoth mutt lay beneath her, its soulful dark eyes on Casey. It tried, without much success, to thump against the floor the remainder of its abrupt crooked tail; somewhere along its life the animal had lost the greater portion of its rear appendage.

"*Aaaroooof!*"

She winced. Goliath's bark matched his size. She scrambled upright only to see the flight of her former customer halted in the parking lot by the chief of police. The old lady flailed her thin arms, her lavender locks bobbing as she gestured angrily.

"Oh, great!"

The officer said a few words, listened to her rant, patted her shoulder, and appeared to charm her without too much effort. How did he do it?

Casey wished she had his obvious gift; it would come in handy around the diner.

Mortified, she turned toward the principal's table. She felt about as adult as she had back in the third grade, but the diner was now vacant. Marcie must have given up hope of a meal even before Casey dumped what was left of it all over an innocent senior citizen. At least her latest fall from grace hadn't had an audience.

A tinny rendition of Beethoven's Ninth rang out from somewhere to her right. "That's all I need."

The only ones who would call her were members of her family. Casey's tendency to cut and run after disaster struck didn't lend itself to building many friendships. Not that she made many friends to begin with; her shyness was a major obstacle.

She rummaged in her bag until she found the small device. "Hello?"

"Hello, dear," her mother said. "Did you get to Eden? Did you have any trouble on the way?"

Only if one considered a close encounter of the bovine kind trouble. "No. It was a long drive but not bad."

"Did that. . .old car of yours make it okay?"

"Yes, Mom."

"And did you get lost too many times?"

"None."

"None?"

"That's what I said."

"I see." After a few moments of silence, her mother continued. "Well, then. How did you find the diner?"

What could she say? "It was right where you told me it'd be—in Eden."

"That's not what I meant, dear. How does the operation look to you? Are the employees efficient? Are you sure you didn't bite off more than you can chew?"

Finally, Mom got to the point. But Casey couldn't, she just couldn't, tell her ultra-efficient, super successful, and über-capable mother the truth.

She looked into the disastrous kitchen via the pass-through over the counter and said the only thing she knew to be true. "I'm fine, Mom. Really. I can do this just fine."

She hoped.

"I hope so." Her mother echoed her thought in a voice with no conviction. "You know we can't let down the Saylors. The diner has to stay profitable for us to get top dollar for them. They need it for their nest egg now that they've retired."

Casey's stomach knotted. "Mom, you told me this at least nine times before I left. I know what I have to do. And I can. I'll be fine."

She heard the door behind her open, and Goliath let out another prodigious *"Aaarooooof!"*

"Casey?" her mother asked. "What was that? Where are you? What have you done this time?"

Rod Harmon stood just inside the diner, Goliath at his side. Casey fought the renewed tears and squared her shoulders. "I haven't done a thing, I'm in Eden, and that. . . that was a. . .a. . ."

How could she explain Goliath to her mother?

She couldn't.

"Casey Elizabeth Hunt! What is going on there?"

She met the cop's clear blue eyes. Her mother's voice grew more agitated, but for long moments Casey couldn't answer, couldn't speak.

Somehow *The most gorgeous man on earth is the only person in the Saylors' diner, which, by the way, is a total wreck, and I'm watching him scratch the biggest, hairiest, ugliest brown mutt alive* didn't seem a good answer.

So instead she said, "Don't worry, Mom. I'm going to be fine, the diner's going to be fine, and I'm in charge now. Don't worry."

Before her mother could object to that outrageous statement, Casey turned off the cell phone. When she next spoke to her mom, she'd hear her full opinion on the matter. But for now, what she needed most was breathing room. And a silent cell phone would give her just that.

She took a deep breath. "What did you need?"

The lawman gave her an odd look, one she didn't try for a second to decipher.

"O—kay," he said. "So you're in charge, as you just said. What's your plan?"

Casey bit her bottom lip. What kind of a plan did she have?

To win some thinking time, she turned to her purse and stowed the phone. "I think I'd better close the diner for the rest of the day."

"O—kay. Then what?"

What was he? Her interrogator?

She shot another glance at the kitchen. "I think it would make sense for me to look at what the Saylors left in the way of supplies. That way, I'll be able to plan future menus."

Yeah, right. What did she know about menus? Other than

the kind waiters always handed her.

"I see." The cop crossed his arms over his broad chest. "Any idea how long that will take?"

"Er. . .it depends."

"On what?"

She shot wild looks at the coffee machine, the counter with its almost empty pie case, the vacant booths. "On how much I have to account for."

"Hmm."

"Really," she said, "I can't know how long it'll take me to get this place back in order. You do realize that the staff—I figure that handful of kids was the entire staff—quit? I'm going to have to hire new employees. That'll take some time."

And buy her some, too.

He gave her a crooked smile. "True. Any idea how you'll do that?"

Casey sighed in relief. This one she could answer. "Sure. I'll call your local headhunter and check out their roster of applicants."

At first he drew his eyebrows together. Then he shook his head. Finally, Chief of Police Rod Harmon burst into laughter, big, full peals that seemed to break somewhere deep inside him and pour out with energy and vitality.

If he hadn't been laughing at her, she would have loved to just stand there and watch him.

But he was laughing at her. "Hey! You don't have to be so. . ." Obnoxious was probably not a good word to throw at a cop. "What's so funny?"

He shook his head again. "You."

She put her fists on her hips. "I'm not funny. I'm perfectly serious. Why are you laughing like a madman?"

"Because, Miss Casey Hunt, the nearest headhunter is about an hour away in El Paso. And trust me, they won't have anyone who'll want to come cook or wait tables way out here in what they like to call the middle of nowhere. I'm afraid you're on your own."

Casey's stomach lurched. "On—my—own?"

"Yup. Either you cook and wait tables, or you'll have to round up a bunch of kids like the ones who ran out of here a little while ago to do it for you. Eden's been losing residents at a pace equal to the graduating classes from the high school. Seems that ranching's too hard for this millennium. We can't get natives to stay, never mind talk anyone into coming here to settle."

Although she could understand the cause for Eden's plight—she had driven nigh unto forever to get to the very un-grand small town—understanding it didn't do her any good. She needed help, and she needed it now.

Where was she going to find it?

The police chief spoke. "You sure you want to turn down my offer?"

"Your offer?"

"Sure. To help."

Him? Her? Working with Rod Harmon? Hour after hour of his endlessly helpful, cooperative, charming presence? Not to mention his masculine appeal?

"No! I mean, yes. Yes, I'm sure." Casey rubbed her damp hands on her gauze skirt and swallowed hard. "As I told my mother, I'll be fine, and the diner will be fine. And I am in charge. You don't need to worry about anything. I'll take care of the diner."

If I don't accidentally burn it to the ground first.

five

Rod studied the man before him. "What do you think?"

"I think," said Jim Osterberg, pastor of Eden's Church of the Rock, in his slow, measured way, "that even though we want an organist, we might have to consider the Saylors' retirement as a nudge from God."

"I can, but what about the older folks?" Rod asked. "Think they can accept guitars, a drum set, electronic keyboard, and a couple of the marching band's trumpets as proper accompaniment for Sunday worship?"

Jim shrugged. "My Bible says we're to praise the Lord with lyres, and they're stringed instruments, like guitars. It also mentions tambourines, and they're percussion instruments. And since trumpets are to herald the Second Coming, I think we should go ahead and see what happens."

"I'm afraid what'll happen is that Deely Billings, Whit Tucker, Bedie Ramsey, and their pals will get up and walk out."

"But they'll come back," Jim said. "They love the Lord, and they have for many more years than you and I put together have lived."

The young pastor then tipped his head toward the activity room where teen members of the youth group had gathered to prepare for the upcoming Vacation Bible School. "It's the kids that concern me. I'm as worried as you about the flight from Eden to the cities. But what do we have to offer them here? Maybe if we give them something that appeals to them, they'll decide to stick around."

Rod shrugged. "They can go away—I went to school in Dallas, but once I had my bachelor's degree, I came right back." He grimaced. "That kind of place has nothing to compete with the real and honest folks in a town like ours."

"I'm from Chicago, brother, and I know plenty of real, honest folks there. The Lord just called me to this church. I obeyed His call."

"I know what I know."

"So because your fiancée cheated on you, you decided there wasn't a single, solitary, sincere body out there, right?"

Rod looked away. "I found phonies, Jim, and I didn't want to deal with them for the rest of my life."

"Are you sure you didn't just run home to lick your wounds? Seems to me, God found Lot in a pretty rotten place. I bet one can find more than just one redeemed soul in Dallas, New York, Los Angeles, Rome, or even Baghdad."

"I get your point. I just didn't find much for me out there."

"So you buried yourself in a dying town in the Texas sand. What's out here for you?"

"Home. That's what's here. A place where people speak plain, they live normal lives, love the Lord, raise good families—"

"And they also leave." Jim shook his head. "I think you're hiding, Rod, and that's not what the Father calls us to do. I don't know His plans for you, but you'd better make sure you figure them out soon."

Desperate to change the subject, Rod grabbed on to the first thought that came to mind. "Well, at least I know a thing or two about real life, which is more than I can say about that Casey Hunt woman who came to manage the Saylors' diner."

The reverend chuckled. "I heard about the day she's had. I doubt any newcomer would feel inclined to stay after all that went wrong on her."

"It did strike me that things began to go downhill the moment she showed up on our horizon. The closer she came, the worse things got."

"What do you think of her?"

"Looks like a long-lost hippie to me. Like she's still looking for that land she wants to get back to—you know, how they wanted to live off the land in communes and stuff. I hope she doesn't think she's found that here. Eden's not ready for the likes of her."

"Why do you say that?"

"Because those so-called hippies are about as big city as they come. She's only in Eden to play at something. I heard her on the phone with her mother. Seems the mom doesn't think the daughter can cut it here any more than I do."

"And yet she's come to run the place." Jim smiled. "Maybe God sent her for our sake as much as hers."

"Don't think so. Doubt she can find even the diner's refrigerator. Not without a map, she can't. Did I tell you I first saw her surrounded by Mort Spencer's cows this morning?"

"What?"

"Yeah. Seems she pulled over to the side of the road to check her map and dozed off. In the meantime, a couple of Mort's cows came calling and one stuck her head in the open window of Casey's little yellow VW."

Jim chuckled. "Must have been a sight to see."

"Oh, yeah. And to hear. The woman was close to hysterics by the time I got there. Doubt she'd ever seen a cow that close before."

Jim didn't respond right away. Instead, he stared at Rod for long moments, long enough that Rod began to itch. What was Jim thinking?

Before he could ask, his friend spoke again.

"You know, this isn't at all like you, Rod. I get the feeling you summed up Casey Hunt by an old stereotype and found her lacking. But you're usually a kind and generous guy. It's only when it comes to Dallas that you turn judgmental. I have to wonder."

"Don't bother. The woman's nothing but trouble. She'll be

out of here before the week is out."

Again, Jim took time to think. "I don't know. Something tells me you could be wrong about her. I've no reason to feel this way, since I haven't met her, but your reaction is too strong. I'll reserve my judgment for a while."

"Suit yourself. But you'll see. Just wait until you see the goofy skirt, the long hair, the fruit-and-nut sandals." Rod shook his head. "I met some like her back in my college days. They wanted to revive what their parents had done years before to skip out of reality. I'm pretty sure I figured her out right. Eden's now got itself its own disaster, hippie style—our very own Calamity Casey."

≈

After the conversation with Jim Osterberg, Rod drove down Main Street to check out the condition of the diner—and to see if a certain yellow Bug still sat out front.

Casey might already have turned tail and run.

At the corner of Sands and Main, his stomach let out a prodigious growl. He chuckled. What was he going to do about dinner tonight? He'd already missed lunch, and breakfast—a cereal bar on the way to the morning's roundup—had long since turned into a forgettable memory.

He counted on the Garden of Eatin' to keep his body well-fed, since every time he tried to cook for himself he wound up with the worst kind of stomachache. The minute he heard Casey say she was the new manager at the Garden, he knew his belly was in for a rough ride.

All he needed now was to see how rough and for how long.

And Jim was wrong. Usually, his friend hit the nail square on the head, but Rod hadn't come to Eden to nurse his wounds; he'd come home because it was home. The place and the job fit him like a favorite pair of worn-in boots.

He spotted the yellow Volkswagen right away. He also saw

Casey come out the door of the diner, turn, and lock up the place. Well, at least she had that much sense.

Something—he refused to take the time to examine quite what—made him pull into the parking spot next to hers. He put the transmission in park, opened the door, and stood. He placed his forearm over the window then called her name.

She stiffened. "Yes?"

"Did you finish your inventory?"

She shrugged and unlocked her car.

That weird something again prodded him. "So what did you find?"

"Restaurant stuff."

"Hmm. . .I see." He fought but lost the battle to kill a grin. "And could a guy hope for a meal in the near future?"

Her big green eyes widened. "As soon as I hire staff."

"O–kay." Looked like his belly was in for a long stretch. "How do you plan to do that?"

This time, only one tan shoulder rose. "Since you said an employment agency was out of the question, then I guess I'm going to have to fall back on the old faithful newspaper."

Rod chuckled. "Better hurry. Eden's paper comes out only twice a week. I figure Miriam's about to put tomorrow's edition to bed right about now."

She turned to look up and down the street. Her long, silky dark hair swirled over her shoulders with her abrupt movements. Then she turned to him again.

"Where do I go?"

He pointed south. "The paper's in the building at the corner of Sunrise Avenue and Main Street. I think you can catch her if you hurry."

In a blur of maroon and ivory paisley gauze, Casey rushed away. Her large leather purse—big enough to hold a week's wardrobe, at least—bounced against her hip.

For the third time, the imp inside teased him on. He

reached into the car and picked up his radio. "Hey, Miriam? Rod here."

His late mother's best friend answered in her gravelly voice. "Gotcha. What's up?"

"You've a customer coming your way from the diner. I know you're about to print for tomorrow's issue, but would you hold off a minute or two? Give her a hand, will you?"

"What's up? Breaking news?"

He waved when he saw her tilt the mini-blinds in the north window where her desk sat.

"Nah. Just someone who could use a hand."

"Sounds interesting. And the reason you're using this contraption instead of walking her over here would be. . . ?"

"Just doing my job, ma'am."

"Don't give me that, boy. I've known you since you broke your mama's rib when you were born. You don't want this gal to know you're helping out, is why. And I have to wonder why you wouldn't want her to know."

"Gotta go, Mir. See ya!"

Miriam Nutley knew him too well, and Rod didn't want to dig inside himself to see why he didn't want Casey to know he'd given her a hand.

It could have something to do with her earlier rejection.

Then again, it could have more to do with the panicked-doe look in those green eyes of hers.

Or he could just really be doing his job.

❧

Casey thought over the afternoon's events on her way to the newspaper office. After she got the kitchen cleaned up, she took a tour of the rear of the diner and made a mental inventory of its supplies and equipment. Just when she'd begun to despair that she was in way, way over her head—again—she found on a bulletin board next to the enormous refrigerator a business-size envelope addressed TO HUNT PROPERTY SALES

AND MANAGEMENT, GARDEN OF EATIN' MANAGER.

She'd perched on the corner of the counter and opened the envelope. The Saylors had written an apology for their premature departure, explaining how their children had surprised them with a cruise that left that morning, and they'd mercifully included additional instructions for the correct use of various pieces of equipment.

Then she'd retrieved the day's intake from the cash register, prepared a deposit slip, hung the CLOSED sign on the door, and headed out, with a sense that the diner's future looked a hair better. At least she wouldn't have to call her parents for detailed directions on how to run a commercial dishwasher. She'd been dreading telling them the Saylors *and* their employees were gone and that she hadn't an inkling what to do next. They would have chalked it all up as another Calamity Casey incident—another failure.

She still had to try out the equipment, and she'd have to do it on her own, thanks to the en masse exodus of employees, but she had time to do so while she waited for her future employees to respond to the ad she was on her way to place.

Maybe, just maybe her luck was about to change.

❧

Before long, Casey came back out of Miriam's office, her stride calmer than when she'd headed off on her mission. Instead of alarm, her gaze now revealed a certain wariness, and Rod wondered what had put it there.

He knew the moment she saw him because she stopped—or maybe stumbled—then came forward, her pace slow, hesitant. When she stood about ten feet away, she narrowed her gaze.

"You're still here? Don't you have anything better to do?"

Was she scared of him? He knew his uniform made certain people nervous, and he often chose to wear only the badge, as he had that morning. But Casey hadn't broken any laws. At least, none that he knew of.

"Just doing my job. Didn't want a newcomer to our fair town to feel lost or unprotected."

She snorted. "You're a little late. The mooing members of your Welcome Wagon took care of that."

He roared out a laugh.

She glared.

"They didn't hurt you—I doubt they would have."

"That's reassuring."

When she bit down on her bottom lip, something stirred inside him. She looked uncertain, vulnerable. "Look, Casey. I know you came to do a job, but I wonder if you know how much it will take. I think you need help—"

"I've been thinking about your offer to help me. And I think I can use your help." She swallowed hard, her eyes cast downward. "But not the kind of help you offered."

This could prove interesting. "Oh?"

Her cheeks took on a deeper shade of apricot under the warm tan. "Yes, well. I noticed how easy it is for you to. . ."

She glanced at him, he nodded in encouragement, but then she looked away before she spoke again.

"You seem to have a way about you that makes it look easy to talk to people. I don't." She shook her head. "I've even botched this up right now."

Rod studied her with more care. That vulnerability he'd spotted earlier blazed from her every feature, her posture, her stance. "I don't think you're doing so bad. I don't know what you want, but I promise I'll listen."

The green eyes widened and met his. "You see?" she said. "That's what I mean. You just said the right thing. I always feel so awkward, as though everyone is watching to see me make another mistake, to make a fool of myself like I always do."

What could he say? He'd already witnessed a couple of those tough moments she'd referred to.

But she went on. "I need to learn how to be more at ease

with people. I mean, I'm most comfortable when I'm alone, when I know I'm not under anyone's microscope."

"Are you some kind of hermit?" That might explain her dated clothes, car, and even her attitude.

"Maybe." She made a face. "But I don't think it's because I want to be that way. To do a good job here at the diner, I need to be different. I—I need to be more like you."

Rod blinked. "Like me? What do you mean?"

"You know. You like everyone and everyone likes you." She waved toward the diner. "Even that poor lady I covered in vegetable soup wound up smiling after you talked with her for no more than a minute."

"I see."

A nod made the light of the sunset dance on her rich dark hair. "Yes, Police Chief Harmon—"

"Rod, please. Or at least Chief Rod."

Again, she blushed. "Okay. Ch—Rod. What I need is help to learn how to do that, to learn—oh, what can I call it?" She closed her eyes, and Rod could imagine the mess of thoughts in her head. "I know! I need you to teach me outgoingness," she said, excitement twinkling in her beautiful green eyes.

He arched a brow, scratched his chin, and smiled. "Outgoingness, huh?"

"That's it."

"And you want me to teach it to you."

Her gaze met his, and Rod felt something shift beneath him. Although his head told him Casey was nuts, the need in her eyes and the plea in her voice made it impossible to turn her down.

"Okay. We can give it a whirl. But I'll warn you, I have no idea how to go about it. I don't even think I know what you want me to teach you."

Parallel lines appeared between her brows. "But you'll do it, right? You'll try to teach me outgoingness. Right?"

Rod kicked a pebble with the toe of his boot. He ran a hand through his hair, shook his head, and chuckled. "Never been a quitter, and this is one whopper of a challenge. When do you figure we can start this teaching thing?"

His question came more from his hunger than any real desire to follow through with her nutty idea. He figured the sooner she felt she'd learned some of that "outgoingness," the sooner she'd open up the diner again. But he had to admit she'd definitely caught his interest with her plea.

Just then her shoulders sagged, and she looked beat. She sighed. "Not tonight. I'm so tired, I don't know if I have the energy to look for the apartment. I forgot to get directions, so now I'm tempted to go back inside the diner and curl up in a booth."

"You don't have to do that. The apartment's right here."

"Here?" She looked around. "Where?"

"All you need to do is walk down the alley by the diner. You'll come out and see two doors out back. One's to the kitchen and the other's to the apartment. The Saylors had an addition built behind the restaurant. You don't have to go far at all."

"Thanks," she said with a sudden smile. Then she reached inside her car, drew out a beat-up duffel bag, the thick file folder Dad gave her with all the vital Garden of Eatin' info, and locked the VW back up. With a nod for him, she headed toward the alley.

Partway there, she turned around. "I really mean it. Thanks."

"No problem."

She added, "I know. I'll cook you dinner to show you my gratitude."

Rod's stomach leaped at the thought of a meal. "I'll hold you to it."

She grinned. "Fine with me. G'night."

"See you around."

Casey resumed her trek to the apartment, and as she went, Rod thought he heard her say, "Thank You, Lord. You must have known I wasn't up to wrestling that stupid map one more time today."

Something told Rod that even with the map, Casey might not have found the apartment. Even in a town as small as Eden, she would probably have gotten lost. Then, more than likely, she would have had yet another calamity to deal with that day.

six

Scritch, scritch, scritch.

The odd sound dragged Casey out of a deep sleep. She forced her eyelids open and looked at the travel alarm clock she'd set on the nightstand next to the bed in the Saylors' guest room.

"Eleven o'clock! What would want to make that kind of noise at this hour?"

She muttered on while she dug through her purse for her glasses. Without her contacts, she was blinder than the proverbial bat.

With a shove, she perched the tiny wire frames up on her nose then heard the sound again. She went to the front of the apartment since the noise seemed to come from just outside the door.

Casey looked out the leaded-glass sidelight. "Great."

Goliath chose that moment to let out his distinctive *"Aaarooooof!"*

Before he could do any more damage to the nice oak door, Casey flung it open. "What do you think you're doing, you great big mutt?"

Goliath grinned.

Okay. Now she knew she'd lost her mind. Up till now, she'd only suspected she'd gone loony tunes with this diner management idea. But now, to think that a dog had smiled?

Oh, yeah. I've gone off the deep end, all right.

She looked out at the critter again.

He tipped his head and gave her another goofy grin.

Casey felt an odd twinge in her chest. She ignored it. "Go!

Shoo. Get out of here. Home is anywhere but in this place."

Her efforts had no effect on Goliath. He panted a little, but otherwise did nothing besides look at her with adoring eyes. And smile.

"If you think I have more cream for you to lap up, you've got another think coming." The hollow feeling in her middle reminded Casey that she'd been too tired to eat. "I don't even have the ruined leftovers from earlier today to share with you."

The dog banged his stumpy tail against the wooden stoop.

"Give it up, buddy. I have nothing for you." Memories of the day flashed through her mind. "I don't have a single thing to offer anyone, not me, and certainly not you."

Goliath whined. It wasn't one of those I-want-to-bug-you-until-you-give-me-what-I-want kind of whines, but rather, it sounded more as if he'd understood everything she'd said and commiserated with her.

She wouldn't be surprised if men in white suits, a designer straightjacket in hand, showed up next.

He cried out again, and Casey shook her head. "Trust me. You don't want to hang around me. Who knows what kind of disaster I'll bring down on you? Now, go!"

Goliath thumped his tail again, let out another mournful wail, and slurped his huge pink tongue over his muzzle. When she stepped out onto the stoop to push him off, he bounded past her and into her temporary home.

"You sneaky rat!" She gave chase, but the dog led her from one end to the other of the small apartment. Each time she came close, he managed to stay just a step away from her grasp.

Goliath had a great time.

Casey didn't.

Then she cornered him in the bedroom. "Aha! To get past me now, you'll have to knock me over. What do you think of that?"

He panted. Not much of a response, but at least he didn't wail again. That sound did something to her innards—something really, really scary. It made him sound lonely.

Like her.

She reached for the dog, and he slurped her hand. As she dried off the slobber on her already dirty skirt—she hadn't bothered to change when she saw the bed—he seemed to shrink before her eyes. He didn't give her much time to wonder what it meant. A moment later, he flew through the air and landed on the bed.

"Noooo!" She looked up at the ceiling. "Why me, Lord?"

At the sound of Goliath's snuffling, Casey glanced his way again. It was then that she knew her fate had been sealed before she'd even set foot in Eden. The dog, who looked like someone had put him together from the rejected parts at the canine factory, pushed and nudged the covers of the bed with a determination that surprised her. When he seemed to have the linens to his liking, he looked at her, grinned again, and wagged his tail.

Casey didn't know whether to laugh or cry.

Goliath jerked his muzzle at her, gave a little "Woof!" and she was sure he'd invited her to share the bed.

At that point she realized she only had two options. The first one had her in the living room, on the couch, for the rest of the night. Although it was a very nice piece of furniture, with soft, comfy upholstery, the bed was much wider and offered a great deal more comfort.

Even with a behemoth plunked on bunched up sheets at its end.

Her other option, the nuttier one, but the one that seemed to offer her a better night's sleep, had her at one end of the bed and Goliath at the other.

Casey couldn't believe she was actually contemplating the possibility of sharing her bed with a stray dog who'd followed her home.

Goliath was the first anything to follow her home.

When he grinned again, her heart melted. "All right, you mountain of fur, you. I'm not that cruel—nor am I that strong." She turned off the bedside lamp and plopped down on her side of the bed. "You just better not snore. You hear? One gurgle, buzz-saw riff, or railroad rumble and you're outta here."

She didn't know how she'd ever carry out her threat, but it sounded good. She didn't want the mutt to think she was a pushover.

Goliath sighed and collapsed into his percale nest. A knot formed in Casey's throat, and her eyes prickled. Maybe this really was meant to be. After all, she was as much a misfit as the weird-looking dog. Maybe they were meant for each other.

She reached down and scratched Goliath's furry head.

He purred.

She chuckled and rolled over. A dog with a cat complex had decided to adopt her.

Before long, she, too, fell asleep.

❧

After a surprisingly restful sleep, Casey awoke more determined than ever. She *was* going to make this diner thing work. It couldn't be all that hard. She just had to persevere.

In the shower, she decided that everyone needed breakfast. Even she knew she couldn't be the waitress, cook, bus the tables, and do the dishes, too. She couldn't plan to serve hot food until she hired help. But it didn't take a rocket scientist to serve up granola and a splash of vanilla soymilk—she'd even offer plain. There was always a purist in every group.

A few sliced strawberries, some cantaloupe and honeydew melon chunks, and bananas on the side ought to satisfy most. Coffee might present a challenge. The monstrosity in the diner's kitchen had given off bursts of steam from the most unexpected places when she'd first seen the thing.

She turned off the water, turbaned her wet hair in a thick

beige towel, and stepped out onto the sage green bathroom area rug. After she'd dried off with another of the plush towels, she turned to the sink and caught her reflection in the mirror.

"What do you think?" She grinned. She'd been reduced to talking to herself in less than twenty-four hours. "Is it time for the residents of Eden, Texas, to improve their diet? Maybe you've come here to teach them the pleasures of herbal tea."

The idea appealed to Casey's social conscience, so she hurried through the rest of her morning routine. Less than twenty minutes later, she walked into the Market Basket and went straight to the produce section. She loaded up on fresh fruit, of which there seemed to be a happy abundance, then set off to find the cereals and grains.

That was where she hit the first snag. The only choice in granola was the commercially boxed kind that tasted—in her opinion—like the box it'd been packed in. And the store only had six of the small boxes. Casey doubted that would make a dent in her customers' hunger.

As she debated the merits—or *de*merits, as she saw them— of instant oatmeal, instant hot wheat, and instant grits, she realized she'd become the object of another shopper's scrutiny.

She fought her instinct to shrink and flee, and determined to start revamping herself into a person with the outgoing quotient of the police chief right then. She turned toward the tiny, wizened woman with snow-white curls.

"Good morning," she said. "I'm Casey Hunt. I've come to manage the Garden of Eatin' while my parents' company finds a buyer for the diner."

Sharp black eyes scoured her, head to toe. Again, Casey fought the urge to run.

"I already know who you are," the lady said in a firm, strong voice that belied her frail appearance. "I just came to introduce myself. I'm Obedience Ramsey—Bedie, they all call me. I've been around these parts all my life, so if you want to know anything about any one of us, you just come find me."

Interesting. "Pleased to meet you."

Bedie made a doubting face and tipped her head to the side. "You don't look like much of a cook, you're so skinny, and all. 'Sides, that goofy, big skirt's gonna get in your way, once you're running around the grill."

Casey took in a sharp breath. "I'm used to my skirt."

With a cackle, Bedie shook her head. "Yep, I daresay you are. But is your skirt used to flitting around a kitchen, bending to clean up messy spills, climbing up a ladder to reach the top storage shelves, splashing around in grease and dirty dishwater?"

Casey didn't think Bedie really cared about her clothes. "I can handle it."

Bedie planted her fists on the hips of her black polyester trousers. "What makes you so sure?"

"I've been feeding myself for a few years now."

"Eating and cooking are two different kettles of fish."

"Well, of course they are. I know that."

"So what are you going to do?"

"What do you mean, what am I going to do? I'm going to feed my customers."

Bedie's sharp eyes measured the contents of her shopping cart. "Seems you're mighty fond of fruits and nuts. D'you figure that'll last a skinny thing like you 'bout a year or two?"

Considering that Bedie Ramsey had the physique of a toothpick with a desiccated marshmallow on top, her assessment of Casey's slender but healthy build seemed a bit extreme.

"I'll eat my share, but it's not all for me. This is today's breakfast at the Garden of Eatin'."

Bedie cackled again. This time, though, she bent almost

double, slapped her skinny thigh with an age-spotted hand, wiped tears from her wrinkled cheeks, and gave out a snort or two in the process.

Casey had just about had it with people laughing at her. "If you'll excuse me, I'll be on my way. I've a diner to run."

"Yep," Bedie said between gasps, "you've a diner you're gonna run right into the ground."

What was it about her that convinced even strangers of her ineptitude? Casey blinked away the tears, but hurt as she was, she froze in place, paralyzed by the misery that filled her.

Bedie pulled up the hem of her pastel pink T-shirt—one that sported a pair of sparkle-dusted romantic hippos—and wiped her eyes. She shook her head.

"Listen to me, girl. There ain't no one hereabouts that's gonna come to a diner that gives them what they can open a dusty old box for. Take it from me, and I do know what I'm talking about, seein' as I'm the county's winningest blue-ribbon cook. They want food, real food."

Casey bristled. "Fresh fruits and cereals are real food—"

"No, no. That's just what them nutritionists and health food freaks want you to think." Bedie brought her skinny forefinger to her lips, signaling Casey to keep quiet. Then she glanced down each side of the aisle. "Come here, Casey-girl, I got something to tell you."

Now Casey began to wonder about the elderly woman's sanity. "I really have to go open the diner—"

"Won't take me but a minute to tell you," Bedie whispered. "You gotta know about this, though. They're all part of the conspiracy, you see. Them food faddies and whatnot."

Casey's eyebrows shot toward her hairline of their own volition. She *really* had to get away. She gave her cart a push, but Bedie reached out and grabbed her arm.

"Wait up, I tell you."

Casey's heart kicked up its pace, but then the ludicrous

nature of her fear gave her some much-needed perspective. At 115 pounds, she outweighed Bedie Ramsey by at least twenty pounds. At five foot four, no great height by any stretch of the imagination, she topped Bedie by about five inches. And if it came to that, she could outrun the elderly woman even in her sleep.

"You listen here, now," Bedie said. "It's them aliens on TV who're behind the crazy diets and stuff. They want every last one of us so weak from eating sticks and bugs—ever hear about them cicadas some dip in chocolate?—that we won't give 'em a fight once they land here."

Now it was Casey who shot looks both ways. She saw no potential help. Had Bedie escaped a mental hospital?

"So," Casey's geriatric captor said, "tell me your real plans for the diner. What you gonna feed us? Not cicadas or lizards or any such fool stuff, I hope."

That brought Casey up short. What *was* she going to feed her customers after breakfast that day?

"Uh—er. . ." She thought and thought, but nothing came to mind. She tipped her head heavenward to shoot up a prayer, but found her inspiration on the placard hanging from the ceiling not ten feet away.

Wow! God had answered that one pretty quick.

"Salad," she said triumphantly. "I'm going to put out a salad bar."

"With?"

Huh? "With salad makings."

Bedie shook her head. "That's just a start you got there, girlie. What's the main dish gonna be?"

"Salad *is* the main dish."

"Maybe for them fancy-pants folks in offices, it is. But it sure won't do for hardworking folks like those around here. You gotta give real people real food."

Casey remembered the gigantic man who'd been wedged in

behind the table in his booth. Maybe Bedie did have a point. But *not* about her aliens. "Okay. I'll serve them something else. I'm sure I have something in the diner. There's the refrigerator and all those cans. I'll come up with something."

Bedie *tsk-tsked*. "You know what, Casey-girl? You're wandering out there somewhere near left field. Maybe them aliens already sucked your brains out from way out in space. Or maybe you just don't know spit about folks."

The woman's evaluation stung. "I don't have to stand here and be insulted. I hope you have a nice day."

"I wasn't insulting you," the old woman said in a gentler tone. "I figure I gotta get your attention one way or another."

Casey turned back and met the concern in Bedie's eyes. "Well, you certainly did that."

The white curls bobbed with Bedie's nod. "Good. Now, you listen up, here. You gotta get yourself a plan, come up with some menus, figure out what you need, when you need it, and how much of it you're gonna need. Then you can start to run the diner again."

Casey bit her lip. Then she squared her shoulders. "I'll be fine. I can do all those things. You'll see. I'll be fine."

"Sounds to me like you're working awful hard to convince yourself of that," Bedie commented, this time her voice as gentle and warm as a fireside blanket. "What you need, Casey-girl, is help."

Casey stiffened as if jabbed by a pin. "I know what I need. Besides, I've already advertised for help. I'll soon be hiring new staff for the diner."

"Oh, honey," Bedie said. "You need more than new staff. You need help—*real* help. The only place you're gonna find that is if you turn to heaven for it. The Good Lord is in the business of helping fools all the time."

Casey gasped. The old woman's words stripped her of all pretense. At least, with herself.

She couldn't fault Bedie for her straight talk. She had been a fool to think she could pull this off. She had no experience in the food industry; she'd failed at everything she'd ever tried before. And she knew Murphy's Law should be renamed Casey's Law. After all, if anything could go wrong, it would at the worst possible time and with the worst possible consequences, as long as she was involved.

Bedie must have seen Casey's weak spot, because she chose that moment to drive home her point.

"That diner means the world to most of us, hereabouts," she said, her sassy tone gone. "You'd better get real smart real quick about it, or you'll be run out of town before you can blink."

Exhaustion filled her, and Casey realized she was tired of running. It seemed she'd been running from herself her whole life. She wanted to stop. She wanted to find a place where she belonged.

She wanted to go home.

seven

We paint a great picture, Casey thought on her way back to the diner. She led the way, awkwardly, since the borrowed grocery cart jerked and bounced over every last crack in the sidewalk.

Bedie followed, her groceries abandoned in the middle of the aisle at the store. "They won't go bad," she told Casey when reminded of her interrupted endeavor. " 'Sides, Mo Diamond wouldn't dream of putting my stuff back. She knows I'll be right back to finish my business."

Bedie pronounced it "bidness."

Finally, when Casey had gone no more than seventeen steps, Goliath showed up from out of nowhere and brought up the rear.

No wonder it seemed curtains, shades, and blinds twitched behind every window they passed.

The scrutiny made Casey cringe. Her natural shyness hated the limelight, and here she'd again made a spectacle of herself.

She did have abundant help this time.

"Casey-girl," Bedie said, "I don't mean to stick my nose in your business—"

Hah!

"—but I can see you're in way over your head. I'm sorry if I offended you. I know I can be a pain at times."

Casey faltered. She caught the cart before it rolled away from her then glanced at Bedie. The older woman's sincerity shone from her every line and wrinkle.

"I been told I have a weird sense of humor, and maybe I do," Bedie continued. "But that's something I need to work on with the Lord. And just so you know? About them aliens?"

Casey narrowed her eyes.

"Well, honey, they're just part of the late-late-late night movie I watched last night. I thought if I could get you to smile, why, then I could maybe get you to listen to my advice."

"A movie." Casey stared Bedie down. "Really, now."

Bedie shrugged. "Hey, it was worth a try. But you turned out to be so serious that you thought I'd lost my marbles."

Casey blushed. She hadn't known she was so easy to read.

Her companion waved in dismissal. "Don't you worry none. I know I sound like a lunatic sometimes, but there's joy to be had here in our journey, even if it's real hard to find sometimes. The Lord made laughter just as well as He made tears. And it's our responsibility to find the one and dry up the other. So if I can make someone chuckle, why, then I've done my job, no matter how nutty this fruitcake tastes."

Casey had never heard anything like Bedie's philosophy, despite years of church attendance and her required presence at Sunday school, Vacation Bible School, and other events held at her family's large church. She didn't know what to say.

Her silence didn't bother Bedie. "But, honey, you got yourself the worst case of the shys I ever seen. You plain shrink into yourself when a body just looks at you. You're gonna have to do something about that if you mean to get anywhere in that diner."

A sharp nod of Bedie's curly white head warned Casey that more homespun wisdom was coming and that it would hit home just as hard as the rest had. "You need to get that lack of confidence right out of your system if you want to make something of yourself in this life."

A tear rolled down Casey's cheek.

"Aw, Casey-girl, I didn't mean to make you cry." Bedie reached into her pants pocket and withdrew an unopened package of tissues. "Here. Dry up and forgive my blunt manner."

Casey dabbed her eyes. "There's nothing to forgive. You just gave your opinion."

"Yes, but I've no right to go around hurting folks, and I hurt you."

"No, it's just hearing what I know to be true that hurts. You were trying to help."

"Well, then." Bedie clapped her hands as if to rid them of dust. "That's that. We're gonna help you get this job done, now ain't we?"

A little voice in the back of Casey's head screamed, *No! You have to do it yourself.*

And so she shook her head. "Thanks for the offer, but I really don't need help. I can do this, and I'm going to show everyone—*you*—that I can."

Disgust pruned up Bedie's face. "Casey-girl, pride's an awful sin, and it seems to me you've got yourself a mighty bad case of it. That's gonna get you in more trouble than not knowing spit about the ins and outs of a diner ever will."

Casey didn't know if it was the pride that Bedie had railed at, or if it was her fear of failing yet again that made her do it, but she gave the old woman a cold look, a brief nod, and pushed her cart toward the Garden of Eatin'.

"It's been interesting, I'll grant you," she said, "and I'm sure I'll see you around town. But now I have to get back to my responsibilities. Thank you, Mrs. Ramsey."

"Just remember," the old woman called out after Casey. "The Good Book says that pride goeth before a fall, and I'm afraid you're headed for a real good nosedive, Casey-girl. If you really want me to believe you know what you're doing, you'll do one thing."

Casey pulled up to a stop again. She took a deep breath and looked over her shoulder. "What is that, Mrs. Ramsey?"

"Oh, go on with that Mrs. Ramsey business."

The "bidness" bit hit Casey wrong, and she stiffened her

resolve. She walked on.

"Just call me Bedie like everyone else does."

It looked as though she'd only get rid of the woman if she played the game by Bedie's rules. "Okay, then. What is that one thing you think I should do?"

For a moment, Bedie just stared at her. Then a slow smile drew even more wrinkles on the aged face. "Tell you what, girl. I'm gonna challenge you—double dare ya, matter of fact."

Uh-oh. Was she really that transparent? Her one besetting fault, besides the shyness—and the calamity problem—was her innate inability to turn down a dare.

"I don't think that's a good idea," she said, her stomach's somersaults an irksome part of her response to a challenge.

Bedie's grin turned sly. "Oh, something tells me it's the best kind of idea, Casey-girl. I'm gonna challenge you to do the right thing and accept yourself some help."

"Done!" Casey grinned in triumph. "I already put that ad in the paper, remember?"

"Pshaw! That's not help; those are employees. You pay them to do what they have to do, all that you can't do yourself to keep your business going. I mean *real* help."

There went her stomach again. "Help is help in my book."

"Help is a gift," Bedie countered in that soft, warm voice that she used so sparingly and well. "Let someone help you, girl. Don't be such a porcupine about it. You might just miss a blessing the Lord's sending your way."

Casey arched a brow and resumed her much-interrupted trek to the diner yet again.

"Hey! I mean it." Bedie had the persistence of a thousand ants at a family reunion picnic. "I love that diner, and I don't want to see it shut down. Let me help. Let Chief Rod, if you want a hunk instead of a dinosaur at your side."

Casey glared back but didn't slow her advance.

"Honey, don't go letting your fear of failure or your pride

hurt you any more'n you want to go letting it hurt this town. We need the diner. And you need the help."

As though she hadn't heard a word, Casey sped up and practically ran to the Garden of Eatin'. There, she let herself in and locked the door. The tears began in earnest.

To her dismay, she found it impossible to lock Bedie's words out of her mind. The old lady had called it like it really was.

⁂

Inside the diner, Casey reevaluated her plans. Maybe Bedie did have a point. After all, she knew the residents of Eden. And, although Casey knew its benefits, granola for breakfast might not be the best way to start her tenure as manager of Eden's only eatery.

Besides, she'd left the cart out on the sidewalk in her haste to escape Bedie's keen eyes and tart wisdom.

She'd have to retrieve the food soon or the fruit would go bad in the Texas heat. But first she had to formulate a new plan.

In the kitchen, Casey turned to the pantry shelves filled with dry goods. There she found enormous boxes of pancake mix and equally massive bottles of syrup in assorted flavors. Could anyone object to pancakes and fruit?

She checked out the instructions on the nearest box of mix and was pleased to find them simple enough.

"Hey, even I can mix water, eggs, and oil. I can also grease the grill, then dump the stuff in circles to cook," she told Goliath, who'd followed her inside.

An easy concoction like that should give her confidence a boost. It could also take care of another minor matter.

After she retrieved her earlier purchases, she picked up the phone. "Good morning, Chief," she said when he answered. "This is Casey Hunt. If you'll remember, I offered you a meal in exchange for those outgoingness lessons you agreed to give me."

A dense silence followed. Then he said, "And?"

"And I'm calling to invite you to a pancake breakfast this morning. It'll be ready in about"—she glanced at the instructions one more time—"about twenty minutes or so. I'd like to serve you a meal today, since you never got the one you came for yesterday noon."

His slow response sounded like anything but boundless enthusiasm. "I've a thing or two to take care of first," he said, "but I figure I can make it there in about twenty-five minutes to a half hour. Will that do?"

She released the breath she'd held. "That'll be great. I'll see you then."

It took no time to whip together the ingredients, and Casey liked the sense of accomplishment it gave her. She especially liked the wise and healthy substitutions she'd made to the original directions.

Instead of artery-clogging eggs, she'd used the cholesterol-free substitute she bought at the Market Basket. And instead of using butter on the grill, she went for the light vegetable oil spray she'd found during yesterday's quick inventory. The high-calorie oil for the batter she just omitted.

This cooking thing wasn't that hard after all. Maybe this was what she was meant to do with her life.

She tested the grill for readiness—the box suggested a sprinkle of water, which did sizzle and sputter the moment it landed, just as the box said—then poured out a dozen future flapjacks.

While they cooked, she dumped a premeasured foil pouch of coffee in the basket of the commercial machine, poured in the amount of water the packet called for, and flipped the red switch to ON.

Back at the grill, she noted the bubbles on the batter, again just as the box said she would. Spatula in hand, she attacked the irregular, amoeba-like portions and managed to flip three that didn't stick to the grill, fold, or break into weirder shapes than they already were.

Four should be enough for the chief, right?

Still, she had gobs of batter left, so she poured out some more. It took her a little more time than she'd expected to wash and cut the fruit she'd bought into attractive pieces, but soon enough she'd filled bowls with the colorful peaches, berries, and melons.

"Beautiful!"

But the acrid smell that rose from the grill wasn't quite as lovely as the fruit. Casey ran to save the batch of pancakes and groaned at their charred bottoms. "Rats!"

She plopped the blackened blobs onto the large white serving platter she'd chosen, but missed with the last one. It hit the floor with a dismaying thud. She frowned. Pancakes were supposed to be light and fluffy, tender and ready to absorb syrup.

Goliath ran up just then. His tail marked an ecstatic rhythm, and his smile seemed broader than ever. Then he sniffed the flapjack. A moment later, he shook his head and snorted.

"It's too hot, you goofball. I can't use it now that it's been on the floor, so you might as well enjoy it. Just give it a minute to cool off."

She turned back to the grill to see that her second batch was ready to turn. All of the pancakes were now pocked with popped bubbles and quite dry. Behind her, she heard the dog sneeze again.

She glanced over her shoulder. "What? You're too good for a flapjack?"

Goliath turned and, head high, tail up and bent but rigid instead of swaying, marched back into the guest side of the diner. Casey glared at the uppity pooch.

"You only eat the fat of the land, like cream, right? Well, you're on the behemoth side of fat, so you're not going to be getting that kind of stuff from me. I won't contribute to anyone's ill health."

She bent to pick up the pancake and frowned again. It was hard as the dog's head and probably as tender as the lawman's cowboy boot. A check of the three surviving cakes from her first batch confirmed her suspicion. They were all inedible.

"Am I glad I didn't dump out the mix," she murmured and then poured twelve more puddles on the grill. "I've got to come up with at least one serving for that man."

She couldn't do much about the kitchen's destroyed look, but she was determined to come up with an edible meal. To her horror, flapjack after pancake came out tougher than the last.

"What am I going to do?" she asked Goliath when he poked his head back in the kitchen doorway. "These things are like rocks, and the chief is due here any minute now."

The door out front opened. Casey fought down the panic and dumped the fresh-baked flat hockey pucks into the trash then grabbed the fruit, a bowl, and the granola and threw a tray together. She went out front and stopped dead in her tracks.

The chief of police hadn't come alone.

"Oh." At least she had enough fruit and granola to feed the crowd he'd brought with him. She addressed the kids who'd followed the man. "If you'll give me a minute, I'll serve all of you, too."

"Nah," said a boy with the black hair, sculptured cheekbones, and warm, bronze complexion of a Native American, "I already ate—we all did, right, guys?"

The five girls and five boys nodded, their eyes on the tray in Casey's hands.

Rod gestured toward the kids. "These are members of the teen youth group at Eden's Church of the Rock. Some of them are also part of my music ministry team. I brought them to help clean up the mess in here."

Casey blinked. "You're going to make these kids clean up that kitchen?"

"No, ma'am," said a pretty blond girl. "Chief Rod doesn't make anyone do anything—well, except drive slow, not smoke or drink—you know, that cop kinda thing. We were just in his office having a meeting about our Vacation Bible School when you called."

A lanky boy, six foot three, if an inch tall, put his arm around the somewhat shorter, though not by much, lawman. "We know Ben set the food on the grill on fire, Miss Hunt, and we figured you'd have a hard time fixing everything by yourself." He shrugged his thin shoulders. "Tell us what to do, and we'll get it all ready for you pretty quick."

Casey looked to Rod for guidance. He smiled and pointed at the boy who'd first spoken.

"Okay, here we go: This is Tom"—the Native American boy—"and next to him are Melanie"—the blond—"Schuyler"—the beanpole—"and Will. These on my left are Adam, Paddy, Alyssa, Jenn, Molly, and Ted."

"Ted?" Casey asked, her eyes on the pretty, curly-haired brunette.

"Can you believe it?" the girl asked. "My mom and dad named me Teodora. Sure, I know it was my *abuelita*'s name, but my grandmother, she lived in Mexico, you see. And besides, that was way back in another century. Who knows what other weird names her friends had back then? Teodora—pah!"

Her disgust made Casey smile, but she stifled her humor at the girl's glare.

"Ted's much, much cooler," the teen added. "Nobody calls me Teodora and lives."

It took effort, but Casey maintained a straight face. "I see. But I don't really need help—"

"You'll be helping the kids if you let them work here," Rod cut in. "Our pastor requires all the members of the various youth groups to perform one service project a month. It's mid-June, and these guys haven't planned a single thing to do."

"Oh," Casey said again, and noted how often she'd used that inane word since she'd left Dallas the day before.

"So," Rod continued, "here's the deal. I'll eat my breakfast, and these guys will pull out the detergent, mops, and brushes. They'll clean all they can, and then I'll pick up a gallon each of primer and semigloss paint from the hardware store. All that black stuff around the grill isn't going to just wash off."

"But—"

"Remember," he cut in again, "these kids need a chance to do their service project. You can't let them down."

She looked at the teens, and despite her determination to succeed on her own, she couldn't deny the brown, blue, green, hazel, and gray eyes that stared at her with silent pleas.

"Okay. I guess that'll work, but you'll let me pay them—"

"No!" they all cried at once.

"Why not?"

Ted snorted. "Because it's not service then. See? We have to do something for someone without expecting anything in return." She looked at her pals, who nodded in obvious encouragement. "You know. Like Jesus did for us. He came and died for us just because He loved us. There's nothing we can do for Him in return, to pay Him back. He has everything. He's, well, He's Jesus—God—you know."

That she understood. She'd learned about the Trinity years ago. But the payment part? She'd always thought all those good works you were expected to do were part of that payment.

She said nothing but gave a small nod. "The cleaning stuff is behind the door by the refrigerator. But be careful—the grill's hot."

Rod looked at the bowl of cereal, glass of orange juice, serving of fruit, and small pitcher of soymilk. He arched a brow. To her eternal gratitude, however, he said not a word.

Casey gestured him toward a booth. "Here. I offered you breakfast, and even though it's not what I'd originally planned, it'll fill you up."

Again, he seemed ready to spew questions, but he did as asked. Without a word, he poured the milk on the cereal, took a sip of juice, and scooped up a spoonful of granola.

Shouts erupted in the kitchen.

"She's gonna blow!"

Casey gasped. She'd heard something similar from other teens the day before. What should she do?

Before she could come up with a plan, Rod leaped from his booth, moved her aside, and yelled, "Run!"

The kids dashed out of the diner but stopped on the sidewalk in front. Curiosity filled their faces, and Casey wished she were again that young.

Life hadn't seemed quite so terrible when she'd only been sixteen.

Now she didn't know where she fit in the world of accomplishments, a world that required competence and success, one where only the strongest and most charming could hope to succeed.

One that preferred people like the man who'd run to the kitchen to save her yet again.

eight

Rod had never known anyone so unwilling to accept a freely offered kindness. Casey was different from anyone he'd met before.

He stole a glance at her from his position under the busted coffee machine.

She was pretty in a natural, earthy sort of way. She wore no makeup or nail polish, and when she moved past him he caught the scent of something herbal. He'd bet it came from shampoo and nothing more.

Casey didn't really need embellishment. Her features were even and well formed. She had a nice straight nose and straight dark brows with just a bit of a lift at the temples. Her eyes were huge and a beautiful shade of green. Most of the time, however, they revealed a lot of apprehension and even fear.

She had a nice mouth and a great smile, even though she used it too little.

The top of her head came to his chest, so he figured she topped out somewhere around five foot four or so in her Birkenstocks. Her curves were nicely proportioned, neither overblown nor meager, and quite to his liking.

Which he'd admit only to himself.

Casey Hunt was gorgeous, even in those voluminous, gauzy skirts that got in her way. He suspected she wore them as some sort of disguise.

He couldn't figure her out. Certainly not why she'd come out here in the first place, much less what made her so prickly and determined to charge ahead on her own.

What bugged him most about her was how much he *wanted* to figure her out.

"Hey, Chief Rod!"

He twisted on his back to look at Paddy. The red-haired star linebacker wiggled the can of primer.

"Can we start?" he asked.

"Sure, as long as the walls are clean and dry. That stuff won't stick if the walls are still greasy and sooty, and it'll be kind of blotchy if they're still wet when you put it on."

Paddy glanced at the walls. "They're as clean as Schuyler's fresh-shaved cheeks. Oh, wait. That's right. He doesn't have to shave!"

A snicker burst from one of the other boys and Schuyler blushed, but the others stared at Rod. Casey also turned his way.

"Paddy," Rod said, "you know the rules around here just as well as everyone else. I think you'd better repeat this one again, since it seems you're having trouble remembering it at the right time."

"Give me a break, okay?" Paddy's blue eyes twinkled. "I was only teasing. Schuy knows I don't mean nothing by it."

"If you don't mean *anything* by it, then don't say it." Rod crept out from under the counter and sat up. He never took his gaze from the boy. "Come on, Padraic O'Rourke, repeat the rule, and make sure it's loud enough for everyone else to hear."

"It's cool," the boy argued. "Schuy's not mad."

"He may not be mad, but you did make a personal comment, and I found it inappropriate and embarrassing. And I'm still the law in this town." The last he added with a grin and a wink.

The freckles on Paddy's nose looked darker over his blush. "Oh, all right. 'The only acceptable personal comment is one that compliments the receiver, and it should not be too extravagant or in any way cause or encourage anger, envy, or jealousy in another.'"

Rod reached up for the wrench he'd laid on the metal counter. "Thank you. And now you may apologize to Schuy."

"He doesn't have to, Chief Rod. It's okay—I'm okay."

Rod shook his head. "He has to apologize, Schuyler, because he broke a rule. And I saw how uncomfortable his words made you. That's the reason for the rule, so that everyone can enjoy our time as a group."

Schuyler shrugged.

"Sorry," Paddy murmured, his ears still a bright red.

"I'm cool," the young giant said then returned to the mop in his hands.

"You handled that very well," Casey said quietly.

Rod turned, surprised to find her so close. He winked. "I just followed the rules, ma'am."

"That's not what I meant. I understand you have to have rules for your groups. We had them when I was in youth group, too. It's the way you made sure Paddy did the right thing and how you didn't let Schuyler deny his embarrassment that's so impressive."

He shrugged. "I just enforced the rules. All part of the job—as a lawman and music minister. Gotta keep the peace."

His lighthearted words got a smile from her. But she still had questions in her eyes. He figured it'd be best if he asked his before she did hers.

"What are you planning to do here?"

The questions vanished, and her eyes took on that scared-doe look again. "I'm not sure. I haven't quite finished with the draft for my plan."

"You'd better come up with something pretty quick. This place is as close as one can get to the heart of this town. A lot of people depend on it."

"Depend on it? A diner?" She shook her head. "I don't understand."

He put down the wrench. This mattered more than even

the busted coffee machine—even if did make the best coffee around.

"The town's population is currently at 7,849, most of whom live on the ranches quite a bit away. When they come to town, this is where they meet their friends and do a good deal of their business."

"Here?"

"You don't have to look so flabbergasted," he said, irked by her clear disdain. "We're not New York or even Dallas, but we also like to get a meal out once in a while."

"Well, of course you do. But this place is—"

"You'd best reserve your judgment for a while." His jaw hurt from how hard he'd had to grit his teeth to keep his words civil. "Not everyone thinks a big city with all its lights, glitz, and lies is the be-all and end-all of the world."

"Whoa!" She raised her hands as if to fend off his anger. "I don't think my comment called for that kind of reaction."

He ran a hand through his hair then shook his head. "I'm sorry. I lost it. All I meant to say is that the Garden of Eatin' is pretty important to us around here. We have to make sure it keeps on going."

"So that's why you're so interested in helping me. You're investing in your town."

He gave her a sideways look. "I guess you could put it that way, but it's not the only reason. I really do want to help, just to help."

"Why?"

"Because you need it."

"No, really. Why do you want to help me? What is it that you really want, besides the diner to survive for the sake of the town."

"That's it. I want to help because I want the diner to stay open and because you can't handle all that needs doing here by yourself."

"How can you say that?" she asked, her nose near as high as the sky. "You don't even know me. You have no idea what I can and can't do."

You'd think I just stuck spurs into her sides! "It has nothing to do with you. I just know that the Saylors needed every one of those kids they hired part-time to keep up with things. And both Shirley and Herb spent every hour of every day here."

"I'm willing to work hard, and I'm sure I'm going to have applicants soon."

"Sure you will. There aren't a lot of jobs available around Eden. But that doesn't change the fact that you don't know how to run the diner."

Her nose went up a bit more. "How do you know that?"

He chuckled. "I was here yesterday, remember? And I picked greens off Cordelia Billings' fresh hairdo."

The blush on her cheeks intrigued him. She looked more like a little girl who'd broken her mother's favorite china cup than a full-grown adult.

"Don't remind me of that," she said then caught her bottom lip between her teeth. She nibbled a bit then added, "You must really hate having me here."

"Hate? No, I don't hate having you here. I just don't understand why you came."

She looked around the large kitchen. He followed her gaze and noticed that the kids were busy with their tasks. Only then did Casey begin to speak.

"My parents own a large commercial real estate management and sales company. The Saylors hired them to handle the sale of the diner, and temporary management services were part of the deal."

"You mentioned that yesterday. But why you? Are you one of their managers?"

She gave him what he could only call a glare. "Why do you find that so hard to believe?"

"Well, because—" He caught himself. How could he word his opinion without treading into the territory from which he'd had to drag Paddy only minutes before?

"—I guess because you don't come across as tough as the managers I've met before."

"Tough?"

"Er. . .office-like."

"Office-like? What does that mean?"

Help me, Lord! I'm only digging myself in deeper here.

"Um, yes, uh. . . You know, the business suit, briefcase, and cool attitude sort."

"I. . .see." Her green eyes told him she did indeed see. "You took one look at my clothes and decided I was a flake."

"No! Never." How did a man keep his cheeks from blazing? "I mean, that's not at all what I. . ."

He let his words die off. He wasn't about to lie to her. He'd never be able to face his Lord if he did. Evasion was bad enough, and he'd already indulged in plenty of that.

Rod shrugged. "I'm sorry. I did form an opinion of you based on a superficial glance. Then I made an unacceptable personal comment. I was wrong."

At her surprise, he continued. "Casey, it's my turn to repeat the rule. 'The only acceptable personal comment is one that compliments the receiver, and it should not be too extravagant or in any way cause or encourage anger, envy, or jealousy in another.' Please forgive me."

She seemed dumbfounded, even more uncomfortable than when he'd first found her at the mercy of two cows, or when she'd learned she would be on her own in the diner— or even when she'd first seen the kitchen in its recent state of chaos. Was she that unaccustomed to apologies?

"Please?" he repeated.

She blinked. "Sure. I mean, of course I forgive you. Why would you ask that?"

"Because I offended you, and Christ calls me to seek forgiveness when I wrong someone."

She cocked her head. "You really do that?"

"Of course. I take my Lord seriously."

Her slow nod and pensive look revealed more than he suspected she realized. "I guess you do."

"I do," he said again. "And that's the same reason I'd like to help, and more than with just that"—he gave her a helpless wave—"that outgoingness deal you talk about."

"Do you mean you feel the need to pay me back after you insulted me? As part of the forgiveness you want?"

She really didn't have a clue. "Have you ever been to church?" he asked before he could stop himself.

"Of course I have. All my life, in fact."

"Then I figure you've heard of the Golden Rule. You know, 'Do unto others as you would—'"

"'—have them do unto you,'" she finished. "I've heard it more times than I can count. So does that mean that you want me to help you keep the peace around here? Because if you do, I'll have to warn you, I'm really not very good at a whole lot of things, and that one strikes me as way beyond me."

He laughed.

He howled.

He hooted, and the kids all looked at him as though they suspected he'd lost his mind.

So did Casey.

"Oh, that's funny," he said the moment he could speak again. "You in a police uniform."

The corners of her mouth began to twitch. For a moment, he hoped and prayed he hadn't offended or hurt her again. But then the smile broke through and a happy laugh followed.

Then the strangest thing happened. The shared humor made him look again into her eyes. And he found he couldn't look away. The laughter came to a soft end, but her smile remained. He felt his own, too.

The moment stretched, and they just looked at each other, as if for the first time. And perhaps it was.

When he'd found her in the VW Bug, he'd only seen the vintage car, her distinctive, counterculture style of clothes, and her artistic jewelry. He'd taken those things and formed an opinion of Casey Hunt.

He hadn't bothered to look at the woman who wore the clothes and drove the car, the woman who seemed more vulnerable than most, who didn't smile much, and who hadn't laughed until a moment before.

He did just that now. He looked at her and saw the pleasure she'd taken from their shared laugh. He remembered the wonder she'd expressed at his response to Paddy, her confusion when she'd faced a living example of the Golden Rule.

She needed help, but far more than just his. It dawned on him then that she didn't seem to know much about love, not the human kind, and even less about that of the Father in heaven. His heart broke.

"That was nice," she said, her voice almost a whisper.

"Yes, it was. You should do it more often."

She shrugged. "I mess up too many times to have a whole lot to laugh about."

"Nobody's perfect."

"Some of us are even less so than others."

"But you're still precious in the Father's eyes."

"Precious?" She shook her head. "No. More like a sparrow that's taken up dive-bombing in God's garden and can't seem to find a way to keep from falling again and again."

"He's always there to pick you up."

"Doesn't He get tired of it, though?"

"He's infinitely patient."

"I've probably worn His patience pretty thin by now."

"Nope. Can't do that. Infinite means infinite."

At that, she gave him another of those one-sided shrugs.

"Tell you what," he said, resolve in his heart. "I'm going to show you how patient God's children can be, and when I tell you that's nothing compared to His patience, you'll know."

"How're you going to do that?"

"I'm going to go ahead with your goofy plan and try to teach you that outgoingness thing, whatever it might really be. I've a feeling it's going to take all the patience I have."

She smiled. "I don't think so. I suspect it'll probably exhaust us all. But thanks anyway."

"You're welcome."

They both returned to their earlier pursuits, he under the coffee machine, and she to her list of supplies.

How did you teach someone how to go from shy and wounded to healed and outgoing? Wasn't that something that came as part of one's nature? What could he do to help Casey?

Rod didn't know. *Lord? I'm out on the range at night, and I can't see clear through on this one. Help me out, please.*

Then he realized what he'd just told Casey. He groaned. Each time he even thought of the word *patience* it seemed like the Lord sent him a test. He glanced at the pretty brunette.

Yep. The more he looked at her, the more she struck him as one of those tests.

nine

Even though she saw it with her own eyes, it proved hard for Casey to believe how much the teens and Rod had accomplished in so few hours.

She had cleaned the kitchen and the floor after she'd closed the diner that disastrous first day. But there'd been plenty to do after that day's fiasco—multiple fiascoes, to tell the truth.

Adam and Will washed down the massive steel hood that loomed over the grill. Schuyler's height came in handy when he, Paddy, and Tom tackled the scorched walls. Then the girls demanded the right to wield paintbrushes, too, so the whole kitchen now gleamed with a fresh coat of white semigloss.

The coffee machine had worried Casey. She'd realized that the steam she'd seen trickle from its various seams and official orifices had not been normal. It had, instead, meant that the caffeine-spewing dragon's health had reached the critical point.

Armed with wrenches, pliers, screwdrivers, and other un-identifiable tools, Rod tackled the silver monster. A flood of dingy water sloshed onto the floor when he fiddled with the machine's underbelly, but before long, she saw him empty another foil pack of grounds into the appropriate basket, and the rich scent of coffee now filled the diner. Too bad she didn't like its taste as much as its aroma.

"Want to try some?" he asked. "I think I've got it back in business again."

"I don't like coffee." She grinned in response to his look of horror. "Don't worry. I have my own hot beverage addiction, but it's to strong English breakfast tea. Help yourself."

She gave him a thick white china mug and noticed the pleasant warmth of his fingers when they touched in the exchange. He was such a confident, alive man. Could she ever become that self-assured?

He winked. "I'll take my repair fee in caffeine, then. Sounds like a perfect exchange rate to me."

"If you say so." She turned to the girls, who'd just washed their paintbrushes in the bathtub-sized sinks. "Would you like something to eat or drink? You've worked hard, and I appreciate everything you accomplished."

"Diet cola?" asked Melanie, her blond bangs so long they almost hid her eyes.

"Of course. The machine and glasses are behind the counter out front. Help yourselves."

"There's something else I'd rather have," Ted said. "I know you put an ad in the paper for wait staff and such. I've never been a waitress, but I'm used to serving meals at home."

The quiet, somewhat mousy Molly gave a shy smile. Casey's heart went out to the girl.

"Ted's got nine little brothers and sisters," Molly said. "She uses a tray to put out their meals, and she's stronger than she looks."

The sassy, curly-haired brunette stood proud. "Just because I'm only five foot nothing, it doesn't mean I can't handle just about anything."

Casey studied the girl. "You know, I think you're right. I think it'd be a mistake to turn you down. You're hired."

Ted and Molly exchanged high fives. "Yeah!" Casey's new waitress cried. "I'm gonna work real hard for you, Miss Hunt. I have a college fund, since I want to go to med school someday. I'm gonna need every penny I can get."

"That's terrific." Casey felt a twinge of envy at the girl's ability to look into her future with such decisiveness—something she couldn't do even now. "I'll be happy to pay you going rate and, of course, you'll keep your tips."

Molly shifted her feet. "Um. . .do you have another position? I mean, I could use the money, too."

Alyssa, an African-American beauty with regal cheekbones and hair in neat cornrows, put her arm around Molly's shoulders. "Molly here takes violin lessons. You oughta hear her, Miss Hunt. She sounds like an angel come to earth."

"Let's see." Casey looked from one girl to the next. "If Ted wants to be a doctor, then I bet Molly's dream is Carnegie Hall, maybe?"

Molly's hazel eyes widened. "Oh, I don't know if I'll ever be that good."

"Don't you do that," Alyssa said with a shake of her head. "Every time you doubt yourself, Molly, you put your chances further and further away."

Casey smiled. "I like your attitude, Alyssa. How about if I hire all three of you? Do you want a job?"

The girl gave Casey a smirk. "Who doesn't? Of course I want a job. If you give me one, that'll be awesome. I've got years of training to pay for before I can become a master carpenter."

"A carpenter?" Casey asked.

"You should see this girl's sculptures," Rod said. "But that's only her hobby. She helped her uncle build her grandmother's new home. It's a beauty."

The girl shrugged. "I like to give people a home of their own."

Casey's heart leaped at Alyssa's words. Before she could stop herself, she said, "I'd like a home of my own."

Rod gave her a strange look.

Alyssa waved toward the rear of the diner. "You have a home. The apartment back there was one of Uncle Marv's first jobs. He did good there."

"He sure did," Casey answered. "It's a beautiful place, but

it's not mine. I'm only here until my parents sell the diner for the Saylors. Then I'm off to. . ."

Where? What? How could she explain her lousy track record to these very focused kids?

She couldn't, so she said, "I'll be off to my next adventure." Even to her own ears, the words sounded lame; her voice lacked conviction.

Paddy approached. "Hey, since you're handing out jobs, how many more do you have?"

"I'm not sure, but I don't think three girls and I can do everything. Do you think you can run the diner's dishwasher?"

The huge youth glanced at the similarly proportioned machine. "Do I have to scrub 'em?"

Casey shook her head. "I read the instructions, and as long as there are no large pieces of food on the plates, you just load them up onto the racks. It's only the big kettles or roasters that you might need to scrub."

He assessed the array of steel pots and pans then turned to Casey. "I guess I can do that. When do you want us to start?"

Uh-oh. She hadn't thought that far ahead yet. "I'm still in the process of evaluating the diner, and that's probably going to take me a while longer. You see, I'm preparing a plan—a business plan. I'll let you know as soon as that's done. But I don't know how long that'll take."

Rod's arched brow told her she'd babbled way too much. She drew up to her full height. "Why don't you all write down your phone numbers on this order pad?" she said. "I'll call you when I'm ready to reopen—soon."

The kids did as she suggested, and then trickled away— but only after each had given her a hug, some more awkward than others. Casey didn't know how to react.

"It's okay," Rod said. Here was yet another person who could read her too easily. "They're just like that. We encourage each other to express *agape* love in our church."

"Agape?"

He nodded and studied her with intense eyes.

Rod's scrutiny made her uncomfortable. "Love? They don't know me, so how can they love me?"

"They've been taught that Jesus asked everyone to love his neighbor as himself, and to show it in a respectful way. Their hugs didn't offend you, did they?"

Casey struggled with the emotions that made her throat tight. "On the contrary. But they did catch me off guard. My family isn't very touchy-feely, and our church is a very serious one."

"Oh, our church is as serious about faith as any other. That's why we take God's commands so much to heart."

"That's nice."

"More than nice," he countered. "It's what's right."

She shrugged. "At any rate, I now have four new employees. I'll need more, but it's a good start."

He looked as though he wanted to say something more but then gave her a nod. "Then you should be ready to roll here pretty soon."

She glanced at the commercial refrigerator, the giant grill, the deep sinks, and the storage room door. "Not quite. I have plans to make."

At his frown, she added, "But I won't take any longer than necessary. I hope to have the Garden of Eatin' open for business in a very short while."

"O–kay." His word of agreement sounded more like a holler of doubt.

"Really, I will be. You'll see. I'll make sure the diner hums along in no time."

"Let me know if you need my help."

"I'm sure I won't—"

"We agreed you'd let me teach you some of that outgoingness. Letting others help is part of it."

She frowned.

"You have to know how to receive in order to learn how to give. Trust me, okay?"

Could she? Could she really trust this stranger who'd already gone so far out of his way to show her kindness? Maybe. And maybe she'd be dumb to turn him down again.

Even if she hated the sense of indebtedness his help left with her.

"I will," she said, hoping she hadn't added yet another mistake to her lifelong streak.

❧

That night Casey got another call from home. Her mother told her they hadn't had any serious interest in the diner yet, but that they were working hard on their search for a buyer. Then she'd asked Casey if she needed help.

"No, Mom, I'm doing fine. I just hired some help, and I'm putting the finishing touches to the new menu."

"New staff? A new menu?" Her mother sounded more worried than before. "Casey Elizabeth, you were sent there to run things just as the Saylors left them, not to turn the place on its ear. Are you sure you haven't made any—I mean had any trouble?"

Casey refused to report the events of the other day, and since she didn't like to lie, she said, "Give me a chance, Mom. You'll see how well I handle the diner. I have some great ideas, and I'm working hard to put them into action."

"That's just what I'm afraid of." Her mother sighed. "Fine, dear. Just make sure you don't get yourself into too much trouble. The diner doesn't belong to us. You have a responsibility to the Saylors."

"I know."

When Casey said nothing more, her mother sighed again. "I have to run, dear. Your father and I have a settlement in about five minutes. I just popped into my office to call and see how you were doing."

"Bye, Mom."

"Good-bye, Casey."

After she hung up, Casey studied the list she'd written up just before her mother's call. She knew she couldn't run the same kind of operation as the Saylors had, but she also knew she could run the diner. At least, she hoped she could.

She'd tried to figure out what new path the place could take, one that Casey could travel without a return of Casey's Law.

Goliath snuffled from his nest of sheets at the foot of the bed. To her amazement, he had walked straight into the shower stall when she'd pointed and told him he needed a bath. He now smelled like a damp, but much cleaner, dog. She figured that was just his way of thanking her for bringing home a twenty-pound bag of premium dog food.

"A fifties-type soda fountain and burger joint would be fun," she told him, "but I don't think that would help the town. And neither would a progressive café with organic produce and veggie cuisine, no matter how much I'd like that."

She nibbled on the top of her ballpoint pen. "A pizza place would be fun, too, but I don't think these ranchers would want pizza all the time."

Goliath said, "Woof!"

"I agree. I have to give my customers a certain variety, and it has to appeal to a large number of tastes."

The ratty-looking dog smiled.

"Oh, you like that, don't you?"

He thumped his crooked tail.

An idea occurred to her. "You know. . .this could work. It would offer the variety we were just talking about, and it would also make the place friendly and casual. I'm sure we could keep the cost of the meals low enough to appeal to everyone, but still high enough to turn a profit."

Goliath's damaged ear tried to perk up like his good one

but failed. The effect was comical rather than sad. He sat up and panted with his super-sized tongue lolling out one side of his muzzle. If nothing else, the dog seemed ready to put Casey's plan into action.

"Either you approve, or I really have gone nuts."

He smiled again.

She gave in to the inevitable. "You tell me. I'm drawing up a business plan based on a stray mutt's opinion!" She leaned forward to ruffle the pooch's topknot. "But you know what, pal? I like this idea, and I think I can make it work."

Casey drew some rough lines, added a couple of arrows, scribbled notes in the margin, then sank back into her pillows, satisfied with her evening's work.

"Well, buddy, here it is." She waved her paper before Goliath's big black nose. "The Garden of Eatin' is about to reopen as an all-you-can-eat buffet with a different theme for every day. We'll rotate the program on a weekly basis—you know, Italian on Monday and Grandma's Special on Friday kind of thing."

Goliath dipped his head, first to the left then to the right. A moment later, he collapsed into his nest again, his smile broader than ever.

"Okay! We both agree. And I can start with my one and only specialty. We'll reopen with a pasta and salad buffet."

Once the residents of Eden, Texas, got a taste of Casey's fab marinara sauce, they'd be back in droves.

She'd yet to mess up a kettle of sauce, oodles of noodles, or bags of tossed greens and veggies.

True, there was always a first time, but something about this idea felt very, very right. She'd met enough of the people of Eden to think she now had a feel for what they would like.

Home. That's what mattered around here.

It was, after all, the only thing she'd ever wanted.

Comfort and welcome. Maybe even some of that kind,

respectful love Rod had mentioned.

Surely she could offer that to her customers. The question was: Would she ever find it for herself?

ten

Three days later Casey and her crew were ready for the grand reopening of the Garden of Eatin'. She had a full staff of eight now, and she and the teens had worked out a schedule that gave them each a fair share of part-time hours and weekend days off.

At Rod's encouragement, two of the Saylors' former employees had reapplied, and Casey had extracted solemn promises from the embarrassed boys to never abandon their job responsibilities again. They'd helped her show the new employees where everything went, and Casey couldn't wait to see how her changes worked.

"Hey there, Miss Hunt." Alyssa, attractive in her uniform khaki shorts and immaculate pale blue polo shirt, threw her arms around Casey. "I'm ready to work."

Casey had started to return those hugs with more enthusiasm, but they still caught her by surprise. They felt great, regardless.

"Molly and Ted are in the kitchen with Paddy. They're going over the list of instructions I put together. Why don't you go read them, too?"

With a wink and a smart salute, the girl went to join her coworkers. Greetings rang out, and Casey let herself relax—but only for a moment.

Today was too important. Her future depended on it.

She couldn't, just couldn't, fail again.

At eleven forty-five, the door opened and in came the older woman Casey had doused with the high school principal's soup. "Hi, Mrs. Billings. Welcome. I'm glad to see you've decided to give the new menu a try." To Casey's relief, Mrs. Billings's hair was back to its original condition.

"Had nothing better to do with myself this morning. Figured it'd be fun to watch the show."

Casey stifled a groan. "I hope you find the all-you-can-eat buffet to your liking. Today's theme is Italian food. Our special is pasta and sauce. The Caesar salad's on ice, and you can help yourself whenever you want."

Mrs. Billings sniffed. "Doesn't look much like a buffet setup. Gotta give it to you, though, it does smell good in here."

Casey's relief left her weak-kneed. "The buffet tables haven't arrived yet, so we're making do for a few days. Please, help yourself. I'd love to know how you like my special marinara."

The plump woman approached the food containers on the counter then grabbed a plate and served herself. She trotted back to a booth, studied her meal, then turned to Casey.

"Looks like red stuff on white stuff to me. Got coffee?"

Red stuff on white stuff? Okay.

"Yes, Rod—Chief Rod was kind enough to repair the coffee machine."

Still keen ears had caught Casey's slip, and Mrs. Billings's dark eyes now narrowed. "Rod, is it? Humph!" She shook her head then *tsk-tsked*. "Go ahead. Get my coffee."

"Molly will be your server today. I'll have her bring it right away."

Casey flagged down her violinist-turned-waitress from the kitchen door. Molly filled a white china mug and headed for Mrs. Billings's booth. When the cup was set just so, the senior citizen took her first bite of the pasta she'd cut into precise, one-inch lengths.

Mrs. Billings chewed, swallowed, then went for more. . .and more. In no time, she was back at the counter, her second helping larger than the first.

"Pretty good, this sauce," she told Casey on her way back

to the booth. "Didn't think you had it in ya."

Casey didn't have a chance to thank Mrs. Billings for the compliment, because just then a gentleman who rivaled Methuselah for age walked in.

"Howdy, there," he said. "Came to see for myself what you done to the Saylors' place. The name's Whit Tucker, and I'm older'n mud."

She blinked. "Please make yourself welcome. We've set up an all-you-can-eat buffet, although the special tables haven't arrived yet. You can help yourself to today's special salad and pasta."

His leather-like skin folded into pleats with his grin. "All-you-can-eat? My favorite kinda place!"

Yes! For once, Casey's instincts hadn't failed her. "I hope you'll be back often then, Mr. Tucker. And I hope you like the sauce as much as Mrs. Billings does."

"Call me Whit, girl. Mr. Tucker was my daddy." He crooked a knobby finger at her. Casey came closer. "Not to hurt your feelings none, or anything like that, but Deely Billings can't taste or smell a thing. Hasn't been able to for years. A horse kicked her upside the head, and she ain't been right ever since. Just look at that lime green outfit she's wearin'."

"Oh." Casey looked at the old woman with great compassion.

"Whit Tucker, are you filling that girl up with all your lies again?"

"No lies, Deely, just the truth, the whole truth, and nothing but the truth. Or are you gonna try to tell us now that Bucket o' Oats didn't kick you from here to Sunday way back when?"

Mrs. Billings swallowed another mouthful of food. "Sure he did, but my nose and tongue are as good as ever. And this sauce is great. Siddown, and stuff your mouth with spaghetti, so's you can't talk such garbage anymore."

Whit winked at Casey. "Ah, well. Busted again. Just pulling your leg, you know. Nothing wrong in that, is there?"

Casey had to laugh. "Not one single thing, Mr. Tucker—I mean, Whit. And welcome to the new Garden of Eatin'."

He, too, piled on the food and hurried off to eat. He set his plate down across from Deely, as he'd called Mrs. Billings, and they munched and murmured in obvious pleasure.

"Looking good," Paddy said when he came out to wipe down the chilled container of Caesar salad. "Told you that sauce was righteous."

"Thanks, Paddy. I like it, and I'm glad you do, too. It seems to have gone over well, don't you think?"

"Oh, yeah." He jabbed his chin toward the door. "But here comes your big, *big* test. Here's Chucky Moore."

Casey turned toward the door and caught her breath. The large postal worker who'd wanted his chicken-fried steak platter with a side of burger and fries the day she arrived had just walked in. He gave her a dirty look.

"You're gonna give me my food this time, aren't you?"

"Of course. In fact"—Casey indicated the counter—"the diner has become an all-you-can-eat buffet. Help yourself."

His wide grin nearly circled his head. "I think I'll do me just that."

The giant then grabbed two plates and piled them both up with pasta and sauce. He left them at the same booth he'd occupied before, and then returned to the counter for an equal amount of salad.

When he sat before all four plates, he looked up at Casey. "You got any coffee? Hot?"

"Coming right up." She couldn't believe the quantity of food he intended to consume. "Enjoy your meal."

She caught Alyssa's attention and sent her to serve Chucky his beverage of choice. Once back at her spot behind the counter, she kept a careful eye on her customers. It wasn't until Chucky moaned in obvious pasta-induced bliss that Casey allowed herself a smile.

"Hey!" the mountainous man said. "This is the best sauce I've ever—"

A loud *pop* cut off the rest of his comment. Then Casey heard a metallic *klunk*. A growing *whoosh* came next, followed by her employees' cries of alarm.

"Oh no, oh no, oh no!" Ted cried as she ran past Casey. "Watch out!"

The *whoosh* grew louder, and Casey felt drops of moisture as she stepped into the doorway. Then a geyser hit her middle with full force.

"Ooof!" She fell on the already-sopped floor. "What happened?"

"Beats me!" Paddy cried from the kitchen. "The faucet just flew off, and the water gushed out. You gotta come look at it. This is sooo cool!"

The water continued to spew out with maybe even more pressure. No longer were there just puddles on the floor; now, a rising tide threatened everyone's shoes.

"Hey!" Chucky cried. "What's the deal here? Can't a guy just come and eat his lunch in peace anymore?"

Casey struggled to stand. "I'm so sorry. We have a plumbing problem. But it hasn't hurt your food, has it?"

"No, but my new boots are soaked. I paid me a good bundle for them, and if they're toast, then you're gonna pay me back."

Boots that size and brand didn't come cheap, she noted as she glanced across the diner's floor.

"Sorry, folks," she said. It took some effort to get to her feet, since her soaked skirt clung to her legs like the skin of an onion. "I'm afraid I'm going to have to close the diner again. I don't want anyone to get hurt."

"Hey!" Chucky cried. "I'm not leaving without my lunch again."

"Take it with you. Return the plates when we open after this is fixed."

"Oh, all right."

He sloshed out, and Casey turned to the senior citizens, whose faces displayed pure enjoyment of this latest form of entertainment, courtesy of her.

"Does anyone know a plumber?" she asked.

The door opened. "Hey there, Casey-girl."

Great. Another elderly person to worry about. "Hi, Bedie. I'm sorry, but this isn't a good time for you to be here. As you can see, I've a problem with the—"

"Let me call my nephew, Louie. He's the best plumber in town."

Whit hooted from his corner. "News flash, Bedie! Louie's the only plumber in town."

"Who cares, you old coot? My sister's boy is still the best there is. Hang on there a minute while I get this toy telephone to work here."

Casey stared, surprised to see Bedie peer myopically at a flip-style cell phone then dial a number. She'd never have guessed the older woman would use such a high-tech gadget.

"Hey, Louie!" Bedie yelled. "Haul yourself to the Garden of Eatin'. Looks like you might want to pick up an ark on the way here, too. Old Noah woulda felt right at home."

She listened then asked Casey, "Any idea what's leaking?"

"Nothing's leaking. It's gushing! The kids said the faucet flew off."

Bedie relayed the data to her nephew. "Sounds good to me." She closed the phone and stuck it in her pants pocket. She turned to Casey. "That's my baby sister's boy. He'll take care of you right quick."

Casey thanked Bedie.

"That weren't nothing," the older woman said. She scooted into the booth where Deely and Whit still sat. "So. Whatcha have for lunch today?"

"Spaghetti and Caesar salad," Casey said once she shut her gaping mouth. "Help yourself."

"It was good, too," Whit added. "Didja hear? The diner's going all-you-can-eat buffet."

Bedie pinned Casey with a perceptive look. "You don't say." She stared a bit longer. "You know, I think that might just work. Got yourself some help, too, I hear."

Moments like this one explained why she'd felt so off-kilter ever since her arrival in Eden. "Several of the teens from the local church's youth group applied, and so far they've done a good job."

"We've done a stupendously super-awesome job!" Paddy said, laughter in his words. "And we even get to watch the water show for free." He worked to sweep the water back toward the kitchen while Molly attempted to direct it toward the floor drain with a mop.

Casey's head whirled at the nonchalant way the customers ignored the flood, which explained why she barely noticed when the diner's door opened and closed again.

"Wow!"

The deep and by now familiar male voice brought her a measure of comfort.

"Welcome to the diner's latest mishap, Chief."

"What happened?"

She sketched out the details then invited him to fill a plate. "We're waiting for the plumber. Bedie called her nephew for me."

"Louie's a good man."

Rod's response gave Casey some assurance. Maybe this would be the last of her problems in Eden. "Go ahead. Try the spaghetti. Everyone who had some liked it."

His warm, caring look touched off something deep inside her. Casey smiled. What would it be like to live with that kind of attention directed toward her all the time?

The longing in her heart grew. It would probably feel like love.

"I think I will try the pasta," he said.

He served himself and headed to one of the few booths where the floor was still dry. Her stomach knotted. What would he think of her sauce?

Why did it matter so much?

She didn't know why it would, but it did matter—a whole lot.

He chewed and seemed pleased with his first bite. "This is good. Where'd you get it?"

"Where did I get it? I made it."

"Really?"

She didn't care much for his surprise. "What? Did you think I couldn't do anything at all?"

He lowered his gaze to his plate. He twirled another bunch of spaghetti on his fork, chewed, and then swallowed. He met her gaze.

"I did it again," he said. "I made another of those snap judgments, and I'm sorry. Please forgive me."

At least this time she knew how to respond. "Okay. And can we agree that you'll give me a chance? No more judgments?"

"I'll try. I can't promise to be perfect—hey, I'm just a guy, with all my faults and warts."

"I don't see any warts," she said before she could stop herself. She winced when the trio of elders chimed in with chuckles.

"Ya hear that, girls? She's been checking out the chief of police."

"Who wouldn't?" Deely Billings said.

Bedie whistled. "He's a hunk, all right."

Deely nodded. "What's that all the kids like to say nowadays? Oh, yeah! You go, girlfriend."

Casey blushed.

The kids in the kitchen guffawed.

Bedie and her cronies beamed their indulgence.

Rod's smile vanished. He stood, dropped his napkin, pulled a few bills out of his pocket, then tossed them onto the table as he turned on his heel. When he opened the door, Casey caught sight of his left cheek. A tight muscle showed through.

The good lawman obviously didn't like the idea that Casey might find him attractive.

But why?

Was she so awful that her interest in him would make a man mad?

Come to think of it, she hadn't had one single, solitary, successful relationship with a guy—*ever*. Maybe she wasn't just Calamity Casey. With her ability to chase guys away, she had to consider another possibility. Maybe she had a touch of Typhoid Mary in her, too.

eleven

Maybe he really was the "dumb cowboy" Melissa had called him when he'd told her he'd applied for the police job back home. He'd also told her he would forgive her flagrant infidelity if she repented, and especially if she left the temptation of the other guy behind in Dallas.

Her answer had cut deep. She'd laughed at what she'd called his closed-minded, small-town virtue. Then she'd told him she would never let him bury her in some dusty desert hole where the nearest mall was a hundred miles or more away.

His own response had been just as dumb. He'd said the mall was less than fifty miles from Eden.

She flung the pretty diamond ring at him and urged him to find some hick back home who'd be forever grateful if he should only think to marry her. She was too sophisticated, too unencumbered by outdated notions of morality, and far too well educated to throw it all away and follow him to Eden.

He patted Tarbaby's strong neck. The sweet mare nuzzled his neck.

"Yes, girl. You're the only kind of female for a dumb old cowboy like me." He gave the black beauty another carrot. "Can't believe I let myself look at that hippie redux like that."

"How did you look at our Casey-girl, Rod?"

Blushing, he spun and met Bedie's laser gaze. "I was dumb enough to let myself think she needed help. You know—she's always got some problem or other going on. She's a Calamity Jane, all right."

"Ahh, but does she make the trouble herself?"

102

"Well, no. But she seems to find it real quick, don't you think?"

Bedie's gaze never left him. "If you really want to know what I think. . ."

She let her words die off. Bedie knew him too well. She was willing to give him the chance to turn down her assessment of the situation. She also knew he wasn't a coward.

"Yeah, I guess I do want to know."

"I think she may be just what the Lord's serving up on your plate."

"What?"

"That's what I said, Rod Harmon. I think she's the medicine the Great Healer's prescribed for you."

He went to object, but she held up a hand. "I got something more to say to you. I think you're her prescription just as much as she is yours."

"No way. She's only in town for a little while, and you know I belong right here. Besides, she's got that weird hippie thing going, and she's from Dallas, too."

"Seems to me you summed her up awful quick there. Are you sure you did a fair job of it?"

"Sure. She's putting across an image, and I think it's for a defense. But it doesn't matter. Not to me."

"I think the trouble with you is you're fighting your interest in her—as a woman."

Here was his out. "Not at all. She says she's been in the church all her life, but she doesn't know much about God. No, that's not it, either. She doesn't know *Him*. So I'd like to help her. I think that's what she needs. To know the Lord."

"Sure," Bedie said. "Everyone does. But that doesn't make any difference to your heart, my boy. I think what's stuck in your craw is that you must've made some stupid old promise to yourself or maybe even to God. I bet you promised you'd never look at another woman who came from a city—no matter what city, and especially Dallas—ever again."

"And what's wrong with that?"

"Well, for one, there ain't any women your age around Eden these days, not single ones, at any rate. And for another, not everyone in Dallas is like—like what's-her-face."

"That has nothing to do with Casey Hunt."

"That has everything to do with Casey Hunt, and you know it."

"Is there something wrong with wanting to settle down here? Besides, if I ever go looking for a woman, then I'll consider one who at least has an idea what she wants from life. Casey's life is—who knows what or where? She couldn't even tell the kids the other day what she plans to do after the diner sells. That won't work for me."

"How do you know God didn't send her here so she could fall for you *and* the town?"

His ears went warm again. He waved Bedie's question aside. "I can't look at her as a potential date. I'm more interested in her spiritual condition. On top of all that, I'm too busy right now. I don't have the time for a woman these days."

"Oh, yeah." Bedie's words dripped sarcasm. "The county's a cesspool of crime, and your social calendar's bursting at the seams."

"I don't *want* to get involved with her. Okay?"

"Don't figure it matters much what you want or don't want, Rod. All that matters is what God wants. Why don't you do what you always do and ask Him to show you what that is?"

He swallowed hard but didn't speak.

In her softest, warmest voice, Bedie landed her final blow. "You're running scared from God's will, and you know it. You're awful scared that Casey Hunt's the one for you, and she's everything you think you don't want. But that doesn't matter, 'cause what you really are is afraid to love again, especially a woman so different from you."

Cold sweat broke out all over him, and Rod couldn't meet Bedie's gaze. He turned and rubbed his mare's neck.

But Bedie hadn't finished. "That horse won't keep you warm at night when you're my age, Rod. Remember that."

Then she left.

❧

The gushing geyser stopped minutes after Bedie's plumber nephew showed up.

Louie made metallic noises under the counter. "Come home to Papa," he said with glee.

The kids groaned. The show was over. But the real mopping up was about to begin.

Louie popped out from beneath the sink. "Yup, the faucet came off just from old age and left nothing in place to regulate the water. Nobody's fault. You got yourself some pretty good pressure here, Miss Hunt."

"No kidding. How much is this going to cost me?"

"Oh, let's see." He rubbed his shiny scalp. "It's seventy-five for the call, and the labor'll put you back about thirty-two forty-nine." He scratched his chin then dove back under. "I'll only need a coupla little things I already have with me in my truck, so I figure parts'll come out to somewhere around—"

"Now you just cut that out, Louis Anthony Frawley."

He stuck his head back out and grinned. "Aw, Aunt Bedie, I was just funning her. You know I wasn't gonna charge her no more'n I always do." He turned to Casey. "It'll be twenty-nine for the labor, and about fifty-five cents for the supplies. It really ain't no big deal."

"I want to pay the fair going rate," Casey said, confused.

Louie shrugged. "That's what's fair. I'm the only one out here, and I've got me all the business I can handle. I charge for my time and the supplies. That's all. This wasn't a big deal."

Bedie placed her hand on Casey's forearm. "He'd have me and Weezie to face if he did anything else."

"Weezie?"

"That's my baby sister, Louise. I was two when she was born, and I couldn't say her name right; 'Weezie' just kinda stuck."

Louie laughed. "Like gum to the bottom of a school desk, she says."

Bedie slapped the tabletop. "So how long's it gonna take you to finish that faucet?"

"About five or ten minutes."

"That's it?" Casey asked. "For all that water?"

"Amazing what a little water can do," the plumber said.

"A little! It looked like a flood to me."

"Well, now," Bedie said, "you got yourself some real clean floors out of it, Casey-girl."

"They were clean. I washed them the day of the fire and then the next day, Rod's youth group kids came and helped me get the place ready to reopen. We cleaned up again."

"Nothing wrong with clean as can be." Bedie left the kitchen. "You know," she called back, "I never got me a taste of that spaghetti sauce. Whit and Deely sure did like it, though."

"Let me warm it up for you," Casey offered.

"Nah. I can tell, even if it's cold."

Casey caught her bottom lip between her teeth. This was, after all, the winningest blue-ribbon cook in the county. What if Bedie hated the sauce? Would that doom her future at the diner?

She waited while Bedie got comfortable in the booth. The older woman took her time and unfolded a fresh napkin. When she'd laid it across her lap, she lowered her head, folded her hands, and prayed in silence. Finally, she curled pasta around the fork's tines.

Her eyes twinkled as she chewed.

Casey smiled. "Good, huh?"

"Nope, Casey-girl, this sauce isn't just good. It's near as good as mine, and mine's won five bests so far. I reckon that makes it pretty near perfect. What's your secret?"

"I use fresh herbs and let it all simmer for hours."

"So do I, but yours has something else to it. Can't figure out what."

"Ah, that would be my secret ingredient."

"Tell me what."

"It wouldn't be secret then, would it?"

"Guess not, but it sure is good. You gonna make it often?"

"Italian Day comes around once a week in my plan."

"Sounds like a winner to me."

Relief flooded Casey. Louie walked up and held out a bill. She paid him, thanked him again, and he left.

"Do you mind if I sit with you?" she asked Bedie. "It's been a tough morning so far."

"And the day's still got many hours ahead for you." Bedie patted the red vinyl at her side.

"I'll sit across from you. That way you'll be more comfortable."

"I'm fine," the older woman said.

Casey wiped her forehead with a napkin from the dispenser. Sooner rather than later she'd have to run to the apartment out back and get out of her wet clothes, but she was just too tired.

"I got me an idea," Bedie said after a few silent minutes.

"Oh?"

"Uh-huh. We have us a dinner coming up for the missions' board up to the church tomorrow night. It's a fund-raiser, you know. I think it'd do everybody good if you come and cook a mess of your spaghetti. The church will make its money, and you'll get everybody to taste your cooking. I was gonna do the main course, but you'd be doin' us both a big favor if you'd do it. Other folks will be doing the drinks, desserts, and such."

She really ought to tell Bedie that aside from chopping up greens, cooking pasta, and making a killer sauce, Casey was hopeless in a kitchen. She should have saved one of her hockey-puck pancakes to prove her case.

Then again, maybe not.

Bedie did have a point. Casey made good sauce. To give the town a taste of what they could expect at the diner in the future was an idea with much merit.

"Sounds like a plan. What time do you want me? How many should I plan to feed? How much do you think each person will eat? And where should I go to do all this?"

Bedie filled Casey in with the pertinent details. As usual, the church's youth groups would serve and clean up after the event.

"It's part of their service requirement," Bedie added.

"I heard about that, and I think it's very nice."

"It's more than nice. It's what God's called us all to be: servants."

"I guess."

Bedie's dark eyes sharpened. "You'll learn more the longer you stay here with us, Casey-girl. And I do believe you'll be here for just the right amount of time."

Casey didn't ask what Bedie meant by her cryptic comment. She was afraid of what the outspoken woman might say.

Her heart a little lighter than it had been since the faucet took flight, Casey said good-bye to Bedie and headed back to the kitchen to help the kids clean.

❧

The word was out. The Garden of Eatin' had become a dangerous place. Either equipment blew up, flames threatened to consume the place, or the customers needed an ark to brave the flood. Casey doubted she'd get any takers the next day.

She figured it made more sense to pursue Bedie's plan than to fight the town's worries, and especially to open the diner with nothing special to serve.

The next morning, Casey met Bedie at the church. The

two women peeled tomatoes, garlic, and onions. They minced carrots, diced peppers, and snipped fresh herbs. After Casey added a measure of her secret ingredient, they took a break and sat on stools at the long worktable.

"Where'd you learn to make that spaghetti, Casey-girl?"

"My grandmother on my mother's side was from Italy."

"Your beautiful, dark hair is from her, then."

She grinned. "And the spaghetti sauce. Can't forget the sauce Nonna used to make."

"Nonna?"

"That's 'grandma' in Italian."

"Nice." Bedie tapped her gnarled fingers on the table's metal surface. "You said *used to* make?"

"She died when I was ten. I still miss her."

"You were close."

"She was so much fun." Casey's memories were sweet. "She always had something good for me to eat when I got home from school, and she could make a dead stick grow. We spent a lot of time in her garden. She didn't care if I got mud on me from head to toe. She also loved to sing, and she had such a pretty voice. She sang me to sleep many, many nights."

"What about your parents?"

Casey shrugged. "They're pretty neat, too. They're busy and successful and so smart they make my teeth hurt."

Bedie chuckled but said nothing.

Casey went on. "My brother and sisters are classic over-achievers. I'm the only one who. . ." She faltered but then took a deep breath and finished her thought. "I'm the only who can't do a thing right."

"You can make—what'd you call it? Killer sauce?"

"That's not much. Look at all the stuff I've messed up since I got here."

"What exactly have you messed up?"

"I almost didn't find my way here. I wandered and wound

up surrounded by a couple of nosy cows. Then I walked into the diner, and stuff's either exploded or burst or burned ever since. And don't forget the broken faucet. Everyone knows by now."

"What do you mean?"

"I went to the store last night to get something for my dinner, and I heard someone say that I'd come to Eden to destroy the town. When he mentioned everything that's gone wrong, it almost sounded plausible."

"Okay, let's see. Did you ignore the directions on the map? Or did you throw it away on purpose?"

"Oh, I followed the thing as best as I could. I had it with me the whole time. I just couldn't make sense of it."

Bedie winked. "Map-reading's an acquired talent. And what about those cows? Did you chase 'em down with a bullfighter's cape wrapped around you?"

"Of course not. I pulled over to read the map, but I was so tired that I fell asleep. When I woke up, the one cow had her head stuck in my car window."

"I see." Bedie's fingers tapped the table some more. "And how about the explosions, the bursting, and the burning? Did you dynamite the place? Did you rub a couple of sticks together and light up a fire? Did you plug some vent holes to make sure the coffee machine would blow? Or did you give that faucet a pair of wings?"

Casey shook her head and smiled. "All of it happened after I got here."

"And you had nothing to do with any of it, honey. It just happened, probably would've even if you'd stayed back in Dallas."

"I don't—"

"That's right. You don't have to blame yourself for any one of these things. Besides, I've seen you work awful hard to fix all that's gone wrong. You even gave those kids jobs. There's not much work to be had around here, and they're blessed to have you hire them."

"That's not exactly what happened."

"Sure it is, if only you look at it from the outside." Bedie's age-spotted hand covered Casey's. "Honey, you need to quit blaming yourself for even rain and snow and a hurricane or two. This is a messy world we live in. Only God's perfect, so all kinds of things go wrong. All that's good comes from our Lord. And the rest? Why, it's up to us to make the best of it with His help."

"You know, Nonna used to say something like that."

"See? I told you I was right and you were wrong. Now see here. You need help down to the diner. I'm gonna make you a great offer."

Casey arched a brow. "And that would be?"

"Me!"

"You?"

"Yep. I'm just what you need to make a go of things. Me and my blue ribbons'll be your cook, and you can keep on doing what you do best: Work to fix whatever goes wrong."

Casey gaped.

What could she say?

What should she say?

twelve

Help arrived just as Casey opened her mouth. She thanked God for His well-timed intervention. Otherwise, she was sure she would have stuck her new purple Birkenstocks in it.

But the help brought along its own dangers.

"Evening, ladies," Rod said, his expression one of trepidation. "My kids—your loyal and lowly servants—are here to do their duty."

Paddy and Ben, the boy who'd been in the kitchen when Casey first arrived in town, bowed low. "We're at your service," Paddy said. "Get it? At your service? We'll be *serving* the meals?"

Did even the kids think her a dunce? "Yes, Paddy. I got it." Casey stood to stir the sauce. "Bedie said you know where the aprons, linens, and silverware are. Would you like to set the tables, please?"

The kids shuffled off, their chatter a pleasant background murmur. When neither Rod nor Bedie spoke, Casey turned.

He wore a look of near horror, Bedie, an indulgent smile.

"Did you want something?" Casey asked him.

"Yeah. Spaghetti and salad and whatever dessert you're having tonight. Just hold the fire, steam, and flood, if you please."

Casey tapped her foot on the floor. "That was a cheap shot, and you know it. You even told me the coffee machine was already spewing when I first walked in the diner."

She counted off a finger. "Then I had nothing to do with the charred burgers on the grill—or the kitchen towel that caught fire, either." Another digit popped up. "As to the flood? I wasn't anywhere near the sink when the faucet gave."

Three fingers in the air, Casey approached Rod. "So you can just wipe off that look on your face. My sauce is great—you even said so—and I came to help Bedie and the church. You can stay and eat, or you can go somewhere else and whine."

All of a sudden, Casey realized what she'd just done. She'd told off the police. She'd never gotten in anyone's face like that before. Where had it come from?

Then, as both she and Rod stood stock-still, she heard a round of soft claps. She turned and caught Bedie's look of admiration.

"Didn't know you had it in ya, Casey-girl, now did ya?"

She blushed and shrugged. "I'm not normally rude."

Rod's blue eyes narrowed. "Well, you sure were this time."

Bedie marched right up to him. "You plain old deserved it, Roderick Harmon. You came in, gave Casey a rotten look, and put on some kind of nasty attitude to go with them fancy boots and new jeans of yours."

"I don't have a nasty attitude. I just call things as I see them—"

"Hot tamales and fire salsa!" Bedie had to glare up because of his loftier height. "Remember that chat we had us yesterday? Well, you're back at it again. Do you even remember you were in the diner well before Casey ever got there?"

Casey's gaze bounced from one to the other.

Rod scoffed. "Well, of course I was. I went for lunch."

"Then by your kind of judgment"—Bedie's pause gave the word its due weight—"you're at just as much fault as Casey here for the blown-up coffee machine and the fire on the grill."

"Now wait a minute, Bedie," Eden's lawman argued. "I had nothing to do with either one of those things. I'd only just arrived and sat next to Deely when the coffee machine blew."

"Had Casey arrived yet?"

Rod's blue gaze met Casey's. Something changed in his expression. Although he spoke to Bedie, he continued to look at her. "You're right. Casey wasn't there. She drove up right before the kids ran out screaming."

Bedie smiled. Then, when he didn't go on, she waved in a circular motion. "Go on. Do what's right."

To Casey's surprise, Rod's ears turned red. "I'm afraid I've gone and done it yet another time," he told her. "I took the easy way out and blamed you for stuff you couldn't have known about. I'm sorry, and I'd appreciate your forgiveness."

Now it was Casey's turn to blush. She glanced at Bedie, who looked on with avid interest. She met Rod's gaze again and then shrugged.

"Up until a little while ago," she said with a crooked smile, "right when you dumped all that on me, I'd thought the same way, so I guess I can't blame you. Does that mean I have to apologize to myself and ask my own forgiveness?"

Rod grew serious. "I think it means you have to ask the Lord to forgive your judgmental attitude, just like I do."

"Huh?" Where did that come into the picture? Casey cocked her head. "You really do have an interesting view of things like forgiveness and all that."

"Would you just look at the both of you?" Bedie cried in disgust. "I've never seen a worse pair in my whole life. Aren't you all worn out yet from all that jumping and leaping to conclusions or all the beating up you've done on yourselves? That sure ain't the Lord's way."

"You're right, Bedie," Rod said, his gaze still on Casey. "And I bet the Lord wants my confession, my repentance, and my forgiveness for it all. Better go put in some kneeling time, I guess."

"Way past time, I'd say," the older woman countered. "Right about four years in the making, I'd say."

Casey had no idea what that all meant, but she did know

there was more here than just Rod's snide remark and her own bluster.

"Look," she said, "if it's okay with you both, I think we'd better leave the soul-searching for another time. According to the clock, we don't have long before we have to start to serve."

Rod turned on his heel and left the kitchen without another word. Bedie watched him leave.

"Boy's got himself a nasty chip on that shoulder, and he'd do himself a truckload of good if he got rid of it quick. Otherwise, I'm afraid he's in for a tough run in life."

Curiosity sizzled through Casey, but she knew that if she were in Rod's shoes, she wouldn't want a stranger to sniff into stuff that wasn't her business.

So she asked, "How do you usually serve the meals?"

She and Bedie worked together like a well-trained team, and the fund-raiser dinner went off without a hitch. The meals looked attractive on the thick white plates, the red sauce shiny and appetizing. They sprinkled seasoned croutons on the salads and grated Parmesan on top. The pungent aroma of garlic bread drew appreciative groans from all comers.

Casey took note of Bedie's easy manner with everyone who stopped by the kitchen to compliment the cooks on the meals. A smile and a happy "thank you" seemed to go a long way. Before long, she made herself respond rather than wait until Bedie did.

Soon she felt comfortable enough to add, "Make sure you come by the Garden of Eatin' on Thursdays. It's our Italian Day now—pasta and salad are the specials."

Some gave her wary looks, but most smiled back and promised to do just that. Still, she knew she had to do something, maybe a bit drastic and certainly soon, if she wanted the diner to survive.

She knew just what it was, even though it would require

a great deal of her. She'd fought it tooth and nail, but it was time she did the right thing.

When she and Bedie doffed their tomato-spattered aprons and tossed them in the laundry bin, she said, "I want to thank you for the opportunity you gave me tonight."

Bedie's eyes twinkled. "Told ya it'd work. I bet there'll be a crowd of folks lined up at the diner for breakfast tomorrow. What's on the menu?"

The moment had come. "Well, Bedie, I guess that's up to you."

"Me?"

"Sure. You're the new cook at the Garden of Eatin', aren't you?"

The black eyes opened saucer-wide. "You mean it, Casey-girl? You really, really mean it?"

The cautious delight in her elderly friend touched Casey's heart. What had taken her so long to give it? She'd like to think that if she'd known how much it would mean to Bedie, she would have offered the job much sooner. But sadly, she wasn't sure.

Casey swallowed the lump in her throat. "I can't do it without you, Bedie. I've been a stubborn mule about it for too long. I don't know the first thing about cooking—aside from pasta and sauce—and I don't know the people of Eden well enough. If the Garden of Eatin' is going to have a chance, then you're going to have to give it to the diner."

Bedie practically quivered with joy. "Wild turkeys a-gobbling, girl! We're going to have us the best time. And we're gonna show all these folks what good eating's all about."

"That's right!"

"Oh, yeah."

"Way to go, Miss Hunt!"

"Hey, Bedie, don't forget your blueberry muffins!"

Casey smiled at the cheering teens. If Bedie's reaction

hadn't told her already, their faces broadcast to one and all the wisdom in her decision. Something clicked into place in her heart.

She finally had done something right.

❧

Casey left the church with Bedie, the kids, and Rod. The teens took off in one direction; Bedie climbed onto her bike and wheeled off. Then Rod turned to Casey.

"Can I walk you home? I've a couple of questions for you."

The moonlight revealed the sincerity in his face.

"Okay."

They took off toward the diner in silence. The lack of strain between them surprised her. Maybe there was something to that "apologize and ask forgiveness" thing. She did remember a Sunday school lesson about the peace that followed obedience to God.

"I really am sorry I mouthed off earlier," he said.

"And I'm sorry for my rude response."

"Can't say I blame you."

"It still wasn't right."

"True."

They fell silent again, and Casey wondered why he'd asked to walk with her. He had already apologized earlier.

"Why are you here?" he asked then. "I mean, really. I know about your parents' business and all that. But I'm curious about you. What made you come out here?"

She darted another look at him and saw nothing more than simple curiosity on his face. "It's awkward and embarrassing to talk about. I guess I can give it a try."

Could she do it? Casey had never before confessed her fears and disillusion with herself.

She took a deep breath. "I've never amounted to much more than a headache for my parents, and I'm sick of doing nothing but mess up everything I try. All of Mom and Dad's management teams were already on assignment. I was their last resort, and I thought it'd give me an opportunity to prove to them that I was more than their mess-up daughter. Besides, I figured even I'd be able to keep a successful diner going. I thought it'd be easy."

"It's clear you've never worked in the food service industry. Otherwise, you'd have known how hard it is to make a restaurant work."

"I'm learning the hard way—as I usually do."

"But why this? Why not do something you know better?"

"That's just it. I've tried just about every kind of job already. And I bombed at each one. This is as good a chance as any to prove myself."

"Are you sure your parents feel that way?"

"You should see the way they look at me. It makes me feel like a cute but clumsy puppy that does nothing but tumble over its own too-big feet, knock porcelain figurines off the coffee table, and leave smelly messes behind."

"I doubt it's that bad."

She shrugged. "I do need to prove myself to them—and to the town now." She stopped and faced him. "I can't let them down. If I've learned one thing since I got here, it's that the Garden of Eatin' is much more than just a place to eat."

Rod reached out and took her hand in his. Casey felt the warmth of his fingers like a balm in the hurting corners of her self.

"You know," he said, "I think you've done more good here than bad."

"What do you mean? Awhile ago you practically blamed me for even the Alamo."

He averted his face. "That wasn't so much about you as it was about me, just like Bedie said. I think what you did for her tonight and the jobs you gave the kids are the best thing to happen in Eden for a long time now."

"But the Saylors could just as easily have done the same."

"Sure, but they didn't need to. They ran the place them-selves and only needed very part-time help. You've hired eight teens, and Bedie, bless her heart, has someone to cook for again."

"Bedie? I got the feeling she spent her time perfecting recipes so as to win blue ribbons."

"She does, but that's not the same as serving someone else. She and her husband never had children, and he's been gone over ten years now. There's not much for an elderly person to do in Eden, in case you hadn't noticed."

Casey didn't say that she hadn't found much for someone in her mid-twenties to do here, either. "I'm glad I could help."

"You've helped more than you might think. We've lost kids and young adults to larger cities in droves. Few want to ranch—it's not an easy life."

"I can understand that."

He raked her outfit with a critical gaze. "I'll bet you can."

She arched a brow.

"I'm just saying you don't see many ranchers in Birkenstocks and long skirts. Look at your hands. Not a single callus anywhere."

"You do have a point. I can't deny it. I know nothing about ranching. And I guess that makes me even more awkward than usual around the people I've met so far. That's why I came up with that outgoingness deal."

Rod placed his palm on the small of her back to encourage her to resume their walk. Again, that rich, soothing sensation spread out from where he touched her, and this time, it found its way to her heart.

She could become addicted to this.

"I'll tell you something," he said. "What you've done up to now will likely go further than any so-called outgoingness I might figure out how to teach you."

"What do you mean?"

"Well, the first thing you have to do to make sure the diner is a success is to welcome your customers. They need to feel it's their kind of place. Now that you've hired our kids and Bedie, Edenites can feel more at ease there."

"That still doesn't change that they see me as Calamity Casey."

He jerked his head around. A guilty look spread on his face.

"Don't worry," she said with a smile. "You're not the first to call me that. Mom, Dad, and the sibs have done it for years."

"I'm sorry. Like you and Bedie said earlier tonight, you didn't do a thing here to have me think of you that way. Maybe your family has a problem that makes them think of you like that."

"Oh, I don't think so. I have a checkered past." She grinned so he wouldn't think even worse about what she'd done than he already did.

He went on. "Tell you what. Your determination to keep the diner running and your kindness to the kids and Bedie will go a long way toward changing opinions."

"I hope so; otherwise, I'm afraid the diner's doomed."

"Give yourself a chance." He fell silent. Then he went on. "I haven't seen you at church yet. Would you be willing to accept an invitation to join us for Sunday's worship service?"

Casey nodded. "I always go when I'm home. I didn't go Sunday because I've felt too embarrassed about all that went wrong after I came. I wanted to fix everything first."

"That was your first mistake. God's house is where you go when things go wrong."

She considered his words as they stopped in front of the diner. "Okay. I'll be there on Sunday. Thanks for walking me home."

"You're welcome."

He fell silent but didn't take his gaze from hers. She wondered if there was something else he wanted to say but didn't dare, afraid he might offend her again. Try as she might, she couldn't bring herself to speak.

An expectation filled the air around them, and for a moment she thought he might be about to kiss her.

But then he turned away. "I'll see you Sunday if not at the diner tomorrow," he said over his shoulder.

"Okay."

She couldn't help wondering why he'd practically run away.

thirteen

"Hey, Bedie! We need another bucket of chicken-rice soup out here. And you might want to check on the chili again. That's going real fast, too."

Casey smiled. "Let's call it a pan, Paddy, okay?"

The football player had turned out to be a blessing in the diner. No sooner did a customer leave than the boy bustled to clear the table, swab it down with bleach water, and then set it up all over again. They needed that kind of speed and efficiency.

Bedie's food had folks swarming to the diner. The woman could really cook.

"Howdy, Casey Hunt."

"Hey, Whit! How're you doing?"

Whit stopped by Casey's spot at the cash register. "Finer'n fine, my girl. This here's the best food I've eaten since the Good Lord called my Maggie home. Tried to talk that Bedie into walking down the aisle with me a coupla times, but she ain't buying."

"Really? You proposed to Bedie?"

"Sure. Man that likes food could do much worse than marrying up with her. But she's kinda ornery, too. I figure it's better to come and eat her cooking here and not have to listen to her yammer at home."

"I heard that, Whit Tucker," Bedie called through the window to the kitchen. "If you don't watch yourself, I can have you banned from here, you know."

"See?" He winked. "Toldja. I'm better off not having to listen to that all day."

Casey chuckled. "Better watch yourself. I've come to know Bedie pretty well by now. She means what she says, and I wouldn't want to lose a customer as good as you are."

"Aw, sweetie," the older gentleman said, "I'd come in here even if it was just to see you smile."

She blushed. Whit's courtliness made up a great part of his charm. "You're a master flatterer, Whit Tucker, but you still have to pay your bill."

He gave a theatrical groan. "And here I thought I'd sweet-talked you out of charging me."

Casey rang him up. As he walked out, the high school principal walked in. Marcie Cambridge was another of the diner's regulars.

"Hi, Casey. I see you have your hands full."

"Not really, just the diner's full. Running the cash register is the easy part."

"I heard you bought fabric for curtains."

"Did you?" It never ceased to amaze Casey how fast information spread through the town. "It's true. They're ready, and once we hit a lull today, I'm going to hang them up."

"Did Bedie make them?" Marcie asked. She piled biscuits and an ear of corn on a plate. She then filled a bowl with Bedie's best chili.

"No, I made the curtains. Tea?" Casey offered.

"Iced, please."

Casey looked around for one of her servers. "Alyssa, could you please get a sweet iced tea for Miss Cambridge?"

Marcie bit into a buttered biscuit. "Mmm. You know, I may never cook again."

"That's the idea," Casey said. She came out from behind the counter to check the quantities in the buffet table. "I'm just glad everyone likes our new style so well."

Deely Billings piped up. "It's a winner. What's not to love? We can just eat and eat and eat, and you only charge us once.

Gotta give it to you. You don't even try to fleece us with crazy prices or anything."

Casey took the comment as high praise. "Thank you, Mrs. Billings. I appreciate your vote of confidence."

"Tell you what, Casey Hunt," the senior citizen said after a good, long look. "Way I see it, you're gonna be around this way awhile, so you might as well call me Deely. Everybody else here does."

Tears welled in Casey's eyes. That meant even more than the earlier compliment. Acceptance had been a long time coming in her life. Too bad Deely was mistaken about her likely tenure in Eden.

"Thank you, Mrs.—er, Deely."

The lady nodded on her way to the door. There, she paused. "Tell you what else. I think you'd best move some quicker with the chief, though. He's gonna slip through your hands if you don't snatch him up before he knows what's coming."

"Mrs. Billings! I do not intend to snatch up the chief or anybody else. Why would you say such a thing?"

"Got eyes in my head, is why." She cackled. "I saw the two of ya sharing that hymnbook last Sunday. Looked real good together, too."

Casey sputtered, but Deely left before she could utter a single coherent objection. Since a newcomer entered as the elderly matchmaker left, it was just as well she'd recovered her power of speech.

"Hi," she said to the middle-aged man in the jeans and shirt of a rancher. "Welcome to the Garden of Eatin'. We're now a buffet, so choose a table, take a plate, and help yourself."

The man nodded. "Stan Garvey here. I hear you've made some good changes, and that Bedie Ramsey's now cooking for you. Came to check you out."

"I think you're going to like it."

"We'll see." He proceeded to study everything in the buffet

table before he even grabbed a plate.

Molly came up to Casey. "He's real picky. Aunt Darla says he's as likely to go hungry than eat whatever she's cooked if he doesn't like the way it turned out."

"He's your uncle?"

"You bet. He's my daddy's brother, and not nearly so ornery as what I said makes him out to be. He just really likes good food."

Casey winked. "Don't we all?"

"And Bedie's is great," Molly added.

"Aren't we the lucky ones?"

Casey thought about her words. Luck hadn't had much to do with the success of the Garden of Eatin's new format. She had worked hard, but everything seemed to fall into place as if by some major plan. Maybe God did care about every last little detail of His children's lives. That nice Pastor Jim from the Church of the Rock had preached a great sermon about that Sunday morning.

"Thank You, Lord," she whispered. "Thank You for Bedie and her wisdom, for the great kids and all their hard work, and I'd better give You thanks for Rod, too."

The police chief had been very encouraging, and from the start he'd tried to help her. In contrast, she'd been bristly and fought his every effort. Now she wondered where her head had been all that time. Were it not for all the help she was given, she would never have lasted this long.

Another customer came to pay. Casey rang up the bill, smiled, and sent her on her way with a "Come back again soon."

Paddy zipped over to the just-vacated table. "Gotta go, gotta go, gotta go with the flow."

She laughed. He was a great kid.

Then she realized something else, something very, very important. She was having fun—for the first time in longer than she wanted to count. Once again, that strange clicking happened, and Casey felt as though another little part of her had just fallen into place. She'd done another thing right.

Since the fast and furious lunch crowd had now dwindled to only Molly's uncle and a couple of other stragglers, she left the cash register and went to the kitchen.

"I just want to say how much I appreciate each and every one of you," she told Bedie and the kids. "You're great! Thanks so much for all you do so well."

Ted came up to her, stood on tiptoe, and laid her short arm over Casey's shoulders. Everyone laughed, but she bent her knees anyway. The girl's arm felt too good to pass off the moment as nothing more than a joke.

"You're a great boss, Miss Casey," Ted added. "We love working for you."

Paddy rolled in a cart full of dirty dishes. "Yeah, and the grub ain't bad, either."

Bedie, her eyes all twinkly and her smile as wide as the Texas horizon, swung a spatula at the red-haired football player. "You'd better watch what you say around here. Them's fighting words, and we're family—God's family. Don't you forget it."

"Amen," Paddy said, serious. "I know when I have it good. Thanks for the job, Miss Casey. You, too, Miss Bedie."

Casey looked around the diner through a veil of tears. She saw a number of good, kind people. A foreign emotion filled her, and she felt as though her chest might burst.

Family.

Yes, they were—in a way. She liked how it felt.

She hoped the feeling would last.

❧

Rod went from meeting to meeting all morning long. To his regret, no one gave him the reassurance he wanted. It wasn't easy to find small companies willing to set up shop in a town most thought was on its last legs.

He wasn't, however, about to stop his efforts.

Someone somewhere had to need a community that offered plenty of space for their needs and a work force ready and eager to be trained. He just had to find that someone.

Soon.

In the diner, the spicy tang of chili made him smile. Casey's changes had given him reason to rejoice. His stomach's prospects were much improved.

A pile of corn bread beckoned, and he filled a plate. The bowls Casey had put out didn't seem large enough for a hungry man's meal, but that just meant he'd have to come back to the buffet for more. He'd have to tell her to provide her customers with bigger dishes if she intended to feed them so well.

He looked around for her but didn't find her behind the counter where she usually sat. He did, however, spot the giant ratty brown dog on the floor next to the farthest booth. Casey had to be near. Her dog never went far from her side.

A girl stood on the table in Goliath's booth, and Rod watched her prod and nudge and tweak a red-and-white-checked curtain into place. Casey must have hired someone else. It struck him as strange that he didn't recognize the leggy, pony-tailed brunette right away.

"Hey there!" he called. "Is Casey around?"

The girl spun. A bunch of pins dropped from her mouth.

He gaped.

"What do you mean, am I around?" Casey said. "Where else would I be? Do you need something?"

He closed his mouth then opened it again. He tried to speak but nothing came out. He swallowed, cleared his throat, and gave it another try.

"Uh. . .you lost your skirt," he said.

Casey looked down.

He smacked his forehead. If he hadn't been before this, he

sure qualified now as the dumbest cowboy around.

"I'm in uniform," she said, as though that explained the change from hippie wannabe to stylish, twenty-first-century woman.

The pale blue polo shirt and khaki shorts suited her far better than the vast, flowing skirts ever had. Casey now looked fresh, competent, and prettier than ever.

"I like it."

"But it's not new. We've all worn the same thing since the diner reopened—well, except for Bedie. She won't wear the uniform shorts, you know, just khaki pants."

"Guess I just didn't notice. You always stay behind the counter." He put his food on a table and walked over to her side. "Here, let me give you a hand so you don't fall. And I'll help you find those pins you spit out."

"I didn't spit them out. You just startled me, and they fell from my mouth. But I'll take your offer. Pins are hard to find, and I don't want Goliath to be the one to do it."

"*Aaaaaroooooof!*" the gargantuan dog said.

Casey's little phone chimed out Beethoven's Ninth. She ran to the register and answered. "Oh, hi, Warren," she said. "Did you track them down?"

Rod focused on the dropped pins, but he was curious enough to keep an ear on Casey's conversation.

"You did?" she said. "Oh, that's terrific!" Her grin lit up the whole diner. "How soon can you get them here? Really? Day after tomorrow is perfect. Wow! You're the best, Warren. I owe you one."

He wondered what Warren had done to earn that kind of smile. Then she laughed, and the sound sent a jolt of warmth through him.

"Okay," she added. "I guess a check will be pretty good, too. I'll put it in the mail this afternoon. Thanks again. See you soon."

Casey spun around, did a little jig of joy, and then clapped with glee. "Yes!"

"Want to share the good news?" he asked.

"I scored a dozen vintage diner stools for next to nothing. They match ours. I want to add a couple more at the counter then use the rest for the outside tables I ordered yesterday."

"Why'd the Saylors decide to expand now?"

She drew in a sharp breath. "Oh. I didn't even think about them. I should, shouldn't I?"

"It is their diner."

"But I'm adding value to it. They shouldn't object. I'm paying for everything, and I only want back what I spent after the place sells."

"I see. And what if the new buyer doesn't want outdoor seating?"

She frowned. "I guess they can always tear everything down, but that would be dumb. I mean, we can handle a lot more people in good weather that way, and I can also hire more kids to serve the added volume. It's a win-win situation all around, don't you think?"

He sighed. "Anything that adds jobs to Eden's economy is great by me, but I'm not the diner's owner, old or new."

"Too bad," she said. "I'm pretty sure I could talk you into all the neat changes I'm making."

"*All* the neat changes? What else have you done?"

"Nothing much. I just ordered new linoleum squares—wait till you see them! Big black and white ones like they used back in the thirties and forties. And you saw the curtains I made. They look pretty nice, don't they?"

"I think they're great. I don't know why the Saylors didn't do it earlier. The place looks much better with them on the windows. It's. . .I don't know, cozier, more welcoming."

She tipped her head and gave him a shy smile. "I was going for warm, comforting, and homey."

He looked around the diner, thinking back over the comments he'd heard since she reopened the place. The common thread that tied it all was a sense of ease and goodwill.

A glance over his shoulder told him his response mattered to her, and, evidently, a great deal. He nodded. "I think you hit it right on the nose, Casey Hunt."

And then, to the shock and surprise of them both, he leaned forward and kissed her pert nose.

fourteen

Later that evening, Casey didn't know whether she ought to run for the hills or just savor the memory of Rod's kiss. What had he meant by it?

He could have used the caress as a stamp of accomplishment. Or he could have meant it as the kind of kiss he'd give a niece or elderly aunt. True, there was always the outside chance he'd meant it as a gesture of affection—the kind that could, maybe, mean something greater than just that light kiss. Between a man and a woman, of course.

She wondered if he'd felt the electric charge that ran through her at their touch. It had stunned her, left her speechless, and if it hadn't been for Bedie's timely intervention—a call for her presence in the kitchen to referee a disagreement between the girls—Casey was afraid she might have made a fool of herself yet again.

That didn't even bear thinking.

Chief of Police Rod Harmon had already seen her in enough embarrassing situations.

A realist, or so she hoped, Casey couldn't let herself think the handsome cop might be interested in her. It would be too easy for her to fall head over heels for the guy. She'd had to admit to herself how close Rod came to ideal.

Decent, upright, hardworking, devoted to his town and heritage, helpful, a pillar at the Church of the Rock, kind to children and animals. . .

He was almost a caricature. Except that, on rare occasions, he did exhibit an unpleasant tendency to jump to conclusions on the basis of a bias. She'd been on the receiving end of that flaw more than a time or two.

Then again, she was nobody's idea of perfect, either.

She zipped up the cash pouch, grabbed her keys, and whistled for Goliath. "Time to head for the bank, big boy. It's almost six o'clock, and I don't want them to close up on me before I make the deposit."

The dog lumbered up, his grin in place.

"You know what that means, don't you?" she chuckled and rubbed him between the ears. "It didn't take Babs Oakley long to charm you with those doggie cookies she feeds you, you thief of hearts. How come you didn't latch on to her instead of me when you showed up in town?"

Casey had tried to find the animal's owner, but no one had seen him before, and no one could point a finger at the person who'd tried to escape the responsibility of pet ownership. She figured the two of them, strays in their separate ways, had landed in Eden at the same time for some as yet unknown reason.

She locked the diner and put the keys in her purse. "Let's go."

The dog's nails clicked against the sidewalk with every step they took to the Bank of Eden. Casey glanced at her canine companion. In the back of her mind a thought threatened each time she thought of their coincidental arrival in town, but she was too much of a coward to let it come to the front.

She didn't want to face what she suspected. At least, she didn't just yet.

Banking done and Goliath's snack devoured, she dragged him outside against his will. Babs's treats presented him with a great reason to stay in the bank.

"Come on, you," she said through gritted teeth.

Goliath dug in his heels.

Casey pulled harder and backed out of the place, her rear end against the glass door. "Liver! I have liver for you at home."

The dog pricked up an ear. She took advantage of his gluttonous nature and rushed him out.

A solid wall stopped her exit. "Oooof!"

"Casey! Are you all right?" the solid wall of masculine muscle asked. The concern in Rod's blue eyes did something to that place in her chest where the feelings his kiss caused now lived.

"Uh, yes. Are you?"

"My toes will live."

"Oh, no! I'm so sorry. I can't believe I barged out and didn't bother to look where I was going, and now I've gone and stomped on your toe—"

"Whoa!" His large, warm hands landed on her shoulders. "You don't weigh enough to feel through the leather of my boot, so you can go easy on yourself."

She glanced down. "Those boots do look sturdy enough. If you're sure. . ."

"I'm sure."

He released her shoulders, and despite the heat of the day, a shiver ran through Casey. It left a nasty sensation in its wake—something like loneliness.

She shook herself. Only then did she realize that Rod still stood in front of her, staring straight at her.

"Sorry—"

"Excuse me—"

They exchanged awkward smiles. Then Rod said, "Are you on your way home?"

She nodded, unsure of herself.

"Can I walk you there?"

Casey met his blue gaze. "Sure. But it's not far, you know."

"Better than you. I've lived here all my life."

They crossed Main Street. "Have you really never left?" she asked.

A muscle twitched in his cheek. *Uh-oh.* What had she done—said—wrong?

"Oh, I left, all right. Didn't stay away for long. Came back as soon as I could."

Before she could stop herself, Casey asked, "Where'd you go?"

"Dallas."

"Really? And you came back here?"

His sudden glare had a sharp edge to it. "Don't understand how a man would care for more than the glitz, glamour, and glory of the dollar-powered big city, do you?"

"Hey! Now it's my turn to say 'whoa.' I just asked you a simple question. Next thing I know, you look at me as though I'm a cross between the Grim Reaper and the Mayflower Madam—and yeah, I did choose those two characters on purpose. The way you looked at me suggested them."

He walked on with long, deliberate steps. Casey had to trot to keep up with his wide strides. The muscle in his cheek now looked like someone had mistaken it for Bedie's bread dough. It stretched and contracted, pulled and shrank with each grind of his jaw.

She stopped.

He didn't.

Casey brought her fingers to her mouth and whistled.

Rod spun. Before he could recover from his surprise, she said, "I think you'd better head back to your cave. I can find my way home, thank you very much."

He didn't say a word, but in the light of Eden's approaching sunset, Casey saw him stiffen further. His fists clenched and released, opened and closed. His jaw gave that muscle a merciless workout.

"Grrrrrrr!"

Casey stared at Goliath. "You just stop that right now." The friendly mutt had never bared his teeth before. She knelt, took the grizzled muzzle in her hands, and forced the animal to look at her. "Just because *he's* decided he wants to act stupid doesn't mean you have to join him."

Behind her, Rod chuckled, a rough, humorless sound. "Ouch. They do say that the truth hurts sometimes, you know?"

She looked over her shoulder. Chagrin had replaced the earlier rage on Rod's face.

"I know it better than most," she said. "I've heard it said about me and my lack of talent and expertise for years and years."

"But it's not true. You don't lack talent. And expertise? Maybe you've never given yourself the time to become an expert at anything. You're young, and to become an expert you have to do something over and over and over again until you learn not to make mistakes."

She cocked her head. "You know? You could be on to something there, Chief."

His crooked smile took her breath away. "Maybe I ought to listen to myself a time or two," he said. "Seems I've made the same mistake about you a couple of times."

"Have you, now?" Casey stood and winked. "Can't say I remember anything like that. It's all the help you've given me that comes to mind when I think of you."

Rod looked down then took off his hat and ran his hand through his hair. "Thanks. It looks like you've learned the lesson of forgiveness better than I have."

"You're a good teacher, Rod."

"I'm a lousy one when it comes to me, though."

"No, you're not."

"You better believe it." He sighed. "Here I've been bashing you for something you never did."

When she looked up, questions on the tip of her tongue, he gestured for her to wait him out.

"It's been brought to my attention, more often than I want to remember, that I've painted a whole world by experiences I had when I lived in Dallas." He tapped his temple. "Here, I know it's wrong, but here"—he tapped the badge on his chest—"I haven't accepted it. I've been unwilling to forgive."

Casey wanted to ask him a million questions, but she didn't have the right to infringe on his privacy. If he cared to share, he'd have to reach that decision himself.

He shot her a glance. "I didn't fit in with the college crowd. I didn't even want to. I wanted to come back home where everything felt comfortable, and I knew what to expect from every day that dawned and everyone I saw."

Goliath walked up and licked Rod's hand. He rubbed the dog's tufted head.

He continued. "Some of the students were okay, I guess. But the others. . .let's just say they discovered the joy of making fun of this dumb cowboy."

"Ouch." She understood only too well. The klutz in the crowd hadn't fared much better than an outsider would have.

Rod's blue eyes seemed to stare at something beyond her, something far, far away. When he reached out, she took his hand. They resumed their walk.

"It gets worse," he added. "From my point of view, at any rate."

She was close enough to feel the muscles in his forearm tighten. His fingers stiffened and his jawline squared and turned harsh.

"I was big and strong and was there on a football scholarship. Didn't realize that feelings were traded as a social commodity among so many of them."

They reached the door to her apartment. Casey leaned back to look at his face in the light of the moon. "Sometimes people aren't nice," she whispered.

"Sometimes they're downright rotten. As long as I kept making touchdowns, I was hot stuff, even though a cowboy didn't quite rank up there with the oilmen's kids. When I blew out my knee the first week of my last year, I became yesterday's news."

Casey's heart twisted. She placed her hand on his chest as if with it she could offer the comfort he hadn't received back then.

He covered her fingers with his. "My girlfriend—fiancée by that time—stuck by me during the surgery, but I guess her patience ran out. She found someone else to keep her satisfied while I was in the hospital."

Instead of the pain she would expect, she only saw anger in his face. Had his heart been broken, or had his pride been stung?

She didn't ask, and he didn't tell.

"I forgave her," he said with a shrug. "But then when I told her I wanted the job here since my uncle wanted to retire and I was a criminology major, she lost it. She'd been willing to stay with me, as long as I played by her rules. Her daddy had a job for me in his company, you see, pushing papers on a desk or something like that."

"That wouldn't have worked."

"She told me she couldn't live this far from the nearest mall." The corner of his mouth quirked up. "Turns out I couldn't live that far from the nearest horse."

Casey remembered the first time she'd seen him. Rod sat that black horse like he was the Lone Ranger. He'd looked powerful, invincible, like he belonged.

She shook her head. "Was she ever blind!"

Rod's eyes widened. So did his smile. He squeezed Casey's hand, and then began to laugh. She couldn't help joining him.

It felt good, as if she were a teakettle and the pent-up steam had just found the vent hole. It felt especially good since she'd realized that she, too, had spent years wishing and hoping to fit in with some preconceived idea of who and what she should be.

"You're okay," he said. His eyes said even more.

Casey caught her breath. Something in his gaze warned her,

but she knew she wouldn't heed the warning. She narrowed her eyes and waited.

Not for long.

Rod placed his lips on hers, and the tender warmth of his mouth stunned Casey. She closed her eyes.

The caress gave her a heady sense of rightness, of belonging, of wanting and needing and hoping and wishing, all the feelings she'd never dared feel before.

In Rod's arms, however, she couldn't—wouldn't—fight them. So she let the emotions run with her, the rich sense of being treasured, the sweet comfort of his sheltering arms, of knowing her feelings returned. . . .

Then they were forced apart. Rudely. Decisively.

They looked down at Goliath, his smile wider than ever, his tail off to one side, bent as always.

Casey laughed. Rod joined her.

"The mutt thinks he found you first," he said. "But I've got news for him. He was nowhere near that yellow Bug when I went after Mort Spencer's cows."

A thrill ran through Casey. No one had ever fought a dog for her before. No one had ever cared that much before.

She gave him a wry smile. "That wasn't one of my finer moments, you know. And you're an awfully good sport. Most guys would get mad if a dog broke into a. . ."

He crooked an eyebrow, dared her to complete her sentence. Casey blushed. She wasn't about to touch it with the proverbial ten-foot pole.

Rod's long finger tapped her nose. "Chicken," he said without sting. "Tell you what. I'll give you time to think about that sentence—me, too."

She sighed her relief.

He laughed. "Trust me. We'll get back to it, and soon. But right now, I think you'd better get inside. I'll see you tomorrow at lun—"

Beethoven's Ninth interrupted. Casey reached for her purse but realized she'd dropped it sometime during their kiss. She reached for it at the same time Goliath did, but the dog beat her to the prize.

"Give me that, you goofball!"

He danced out of her reach, his smile in place.

"Goliath, heel!"

A "do-I-really-have-to?" look appeared on his face, and he groaned. Casey lunged. She grabbed the purse, but he refused to release the strap.

Beethoven ninthed away.

"Hey, it could be important, you crazy dog, you." She got her hand inside the leather sack, grabbed the phone, flipped it open, and said a breathless "Hello!"

"Casey! What's wrong?" Her mother's perennial greeting.

"Nothing."

Goliath yanked on the bag. The strap lassoed Casey's forearm. "Oh, no—oof!"

She landed on her face. The phone skittered to one side, Goliath danced off to the other. Her mother's anxious questions shrilled into the brilliant desert twilight.

"Great," Casey muttered on her way back up. "You sure do know how to choose your moments, Goliath."

Rod handed her the phone. A twitch played at the corners of his mouth.

She shook her head and rolled her eyes.

He laughed and went after the dog.

"Yes, Mom, I'm fine," she said when she finally cut in. "It was nothing. I just tripped over Goliath."

"Goliath?"

How to explain the behemoth mutt of Eden, Texas? "Big dog. Never mind him. Did you need something?"

"I just had a most disturbing conversation, one that brought up a number of questions."

She could tell this was not going to be good. Come to think of it, few of her conversations with her mom ever were. She figured she'd be better off if she got it over with soon.

"What kind of questions, Mom?"

"What have you done to the Saylors' diner, Casey Elizabeth Hunt?"

Casey waited. It was always best to know all her mother had on her before she answered.

"And what's this I hear about you making a hundred-year-old lady clean up after your messes? How could you, Casey? I know you've had your share of trouble, more than your share, actually, but this. . ."

A knot filled Casey's throat. How could her mother get it so wrong?

Or was she the one who'd gotten it wrong?

Mom went on. "How am I going to hold my head up, child? My own daughter. Involved in elder abuse."

Casey folded up her cell phone and then turned it off. There was nothing to say. True, she was a klutz and a mess, and Murphy didn't have a thing on her when it came to calamity-dependent laws, but cruelty?

If her mother thought her capable of such a nasty thing, then there really was nothing more to say.

fifteen

Rod took the phone from her hand. He pushed the ON button, hit a couple of others, and before she could stop him, he said, "Mrs. Hunt?"

She glared at him through the veil of tears. She shook her head so hard her ponytail whipped her cheeks.

He ignored her. "I know this is unexpected," he said, "but Casey's phone went off. I turned it on again and dialed you back."

Her mother squawked on the other end. It didn't seem to affect Rod. "No, no," he said. "Nothing's wrong here. Please let me introduce myself. I'm Rod Harmon, the chief of police in Eden, and the P.D. is just down the street from the Garden of Eatin'."

Casey poked his chest. "I can't believe you told her you're a cop! That'll only make things worse."

His smile grew broader. "Of course, Casey's not in trouble. On the contrary. Your daughter's the best thing that's happened to Eden, Texas, in a long time."

Casey shook her head. "Is Pinocchio your middle name?"

Rod chuckled. "Why am I here with her? Well, I walked her home from the bank where she made her daily deposit, and I was about to. . ."

For a moment, Casey thought he'd finally realized how deep a hole he'd dug. Then he winked.

"I was about to tell your daughter she's about to be honored as Eden's Citizen of the Month."

Casey gaped.

"I'll be happy to tell you why," he said. His index finger

141

curved under Casey's chin and pushed up. She closed her mouth.

He continued. "Well, ma'am, since she arrived in town, she's been like a ray of sunshine."

She made a gagging gesture; he grinned some more.

"Casey has made friends with everyone in town," he added, serious now. "And she's done it with her goodness and the kindness she's shown many of our folks here. Take Bedie— Obedience Ramsey—for example."

Casey yelped. "What are you doing?" She went for the phone, but his long arm kept it out of reach. "Give me that thing. You're making things worse. Mom already thinks I'm abusing Bedie. She thinks I've made her clean up after my messes. And someone told her Bedie's a hundred years old!"

Rod covered the mouthpiece with a hand to muffle his laughter. "Oh, Bedie's not going to like that!" He laid his other hand on Casey's shoulder. "Trust me?"

Casey caught her breath. Those blue eyes asked more than to let him continue his crazy talk with her mom. Something told her this was one of those life-changing moments she'd better get right. Her answer meant a great deal—to him, as well as to her.

Did she trust Rod Harmon?

"Yes," she whispered. "Yes, I do, Rod. I do trust you."

He turned up the intensity in his gaze. Casey felt it as though he'd reached out and touched her cheek, the curve of her jaw, the length of her neck.

"Thanks." His voice came out rough, so he cleared his throat. Then he said, "Mrs. Hunt? I'm sorry. I—uh—something distracted me. But as I was saying, Casey offered Bedie Ramsey a job in the diner. Although I suspect there was a fair amount of cajoling on Bedie's part to get Casey to make the offer. Bedie's the best cook around here, and she's been very lonely since her husband died years ago. Since then, she's fought cancer and depression, and we haven't seen her this happy in ages."

"I didn't know it meant so much to her," Casey murmured.

He shrugged. "Oh, no, ma'am. Bedie's not a hundred years old. I'm not sure just how old she is, but it's absolutely not a hundred. Believe me, we'd all know it if she'd hit that mark."

Against her better judgment, Casey chuckled. Bedie would indeed let the whole world know if she'd made it that far.

"Oh, no," Rod said. "Bedie's not the only one to benefit from Casey's generosity. We're a ranching community and have very little commerce in these parts. Jobs are scarce. It's a real problem for our teens who tend to drop out of school and head for cities with jobs to offer. So when she hired eight of our kids, she did us all a favor. Anything that cuts down on our teen unemployment's a real blessing for this town."

Casey tipped her head. She hadn't looked at her crew that way, but put like this, maybe Rod did have a point.

"I see you've heard about the improvements she's made." He waggled his eyebrows. *Now* she was in trouble.

"Well, ma'am," he went on, his steps just long enough to keep him beyond her reach, "I have to say that everyone's pleased with what she's done. The diner looks much better than it did before the Saylors left, and she's made some investments that are sure to pay off in increased revenue."

Casey winced at her mother's wild gibberish.

Rod answered in a calm, sure voice. "No, no. She's not a bit wild or crazy. In fact, she told me earlier today about her thoughtful decision to add outdoor tables. I'm sure you can see how that benefits the diner: More tables mean more customers; more customers mean more jobs and more income; more income means a more attractive bottom line; a more attractive bottom line means you'll get a better price when you close the deal. She's a savvy businesswoman."

That did it. The tears poured down Casey's cheeks. She couldn't believe he'd come to her defense like that—of all people, Rod Harmon. The way he'd woven the details of her ignominious tenure in Eden made the tale sound much better than it was, much better, at any rate, than how she saw it.

Who was right?

His voice cut into her thoughts. "You know, Mrs. Hunt, you really should come out to Eden and take a look for yourself. Casey's made some terrific improvements to one of Eden's most important establishments."

Casey covered her mouth with her fist, the horror too great for her. Mom? Here?

She shook her head again, and this time, even the sting of her hair against her face couldn't stop her. "No! She can't come here. She'll fire me."

And she didn't *want* to leave.

The realization stunned her. Could it be true?

He mouthed, "It's okay. I promise."

Casey didn't believe him. Even though she did trust him. And although she didn't quite know how the two went together, she just knew they somehow did.

"Well, ma'am," he said yet again in his easy drawl, "I sure hope you can make it out here real soon. I just know you'll be pleasantly surprised. It's been a pleasure talking with you, and I hope we can meet sometime in the near future."

He finally closed the phone. He held the troublesome device out to her, but Casey wanted nothing to do with it. She shook her head. He stuck it in his shirt pocket.

"How could you?" she said around the sobs. "You've ruined everything. Citizen of the Month? What kind of garbage is that?"

"It's not garbage, Casey Hunt. And I did ask you to trust me. You said you would, didn't you?"

She gave him a reluctant nod.

"Well, then, you sure don't know how to trust real well, now, do you?"

A rapid-fire collage of memories flew through her mind. "I haven't had many chances to do so."

"It's about time you tried it—for real." He grabbed her hand and tugged.

Casey gave him a hard look. "What more do you want? You've made a mess for me with my mother, and this time, even though I'll have to clean it up, it wasn't my fault."

"You said you trusted me."

"What are you, a broken record?"

"If that's what it'll take, then I'm going to play this song over and over and over again until you get it right. Come on."

"Where do you think you're taking me?"

"I don't think, I know where I'm taking you. And if you don't trust me"—he sent her another visual plea—"then you'll really make a mess of things. I won't be able to help you then."

"I don't need your help—"

He cut off her words with his lips. Casey tried to twist away, but the sweetness of his kiss stilled her. If this was how the man put an end to an argument, she might develop an argumentative streak real quick.

A moment later, he pulled away. "Please, Casey. Trust me. It means a great deal to me."

What woman could refuse? "You know, crazy as it seems, I do trust you."

His gaze went even more warm and mellow. "Thanks. I promise everything will be all right. But you'll have to trust me for a little while longer."

"Okay."

He tugged on her hand again, and this time she let him lead her down the street. A couple of minutes later, they stood outside the Eden P.D. "Why are we here?"

He arched a brow. "You said you trusted me."

"Yeah, but that doesn't mean I'm going to let you lock

me up or anything like that. Especially since you're the one who lied."

"I did not."

"You sure did."

"When?"

"Just a while ago."

"That's no answer."

"It's the one you're getting."

He ground his teeth—at least, that's what it looked like from the side. "Please tell me when I lied," he said, his words clipped. "I need to apologize if I did. I *don't* lie."

Casey crossed her arms over her chest. "You lied to my mother." At his renewed look of outrage, she held up a hand. "You told her all that stuff about how I was Eden's Citizen of the Month. You know better than I do that the town has no such honor and that I'm no one's idea of a model citizen."

"Aha!" He flung open the door. "That's where you're wrong." He crossed to his desk, took a sheet of paper from a notebook and a pen from a holder, and sat in the large swivel chair. "From this moment on, Eden does indeed have a Citizen of the Month award, and you're our first."

At her sputters, he waggled the pen. "Watch me write the proclamation, Casey Hunt."

To her shocked amazement, he did just that. Once done, he stood and thrust the page at her. "See? Here's the first step. Now you'll have to push that wimpy trust of yours a little further still."

Tear again filled her eyes. "What more do you want?"

"I just want you to trust me."

"Why does it matter so much?"

"Because I'm not dumb, because I'm not some kind of hick out in the sticks, and because I care. I care about you, Casey, and I'd never do anything to hurt you." His blue eyes sought hers. "Do you believe that?"

"I believe that's what you think."

"Not good enough by a long shot. You've got to do better than that. Do you honestly think I'd go out of my way to do you wrong? After all the times and ways I've tried to help?"

She winced. "If you put it that way, I guess I have to believe you, don't I?"

"That's what I tried to tell you all along." He reached out a hand. This time she took it without hesitation, and they left the P.D. Goliath's claws clicked on the sidewalk at their side.

"Where are you taking me?" Casey asked minutes later.

"We're here."

They stood outside the newspaper office. She could hear Miriam Nutley's equipment chug out the next edition of the town's weekly. "Here? Why are we here?"

He stuck his fists on his slim hips, making the scribbled proclamation in his hand a white exclamation mark against the tan of his uniform pants and the red of the building's bricks. "What good's a proclamation if nobody reads it? We're here to stop the presses."

Rod opened the door then turned back to her. "Literally. Mir's a stickler for deadlines. We have to hurry if we're going to get this tidbit in this latest issue."

Casey's thoughts spun so fast she felt dizzy. This man was something else—what, she didn't know, since she'd never met anyone quite like him.

And she'd never before felt quite like this. To begin with, this was the first time she'd made the front page of a newspaper. At least it was the first time she'd made the front page of a newspaper for something that didn't entail mayhem, disaster, or humiliation.

Maybe her lot in life had taken a turn for the better.

Then again, she couldn't count on that.

Regardless, she took the chance to do something she'd seen done on TV and in movies and had always wanted to do. Inside the newspaper's office, she glanced at Rod, who winked, then looked for Miriam. She found the owner and publisher of the paper by a massive machine that spewed finished newsprint at an impressive rate.

With an impish grin, Casey bellowed, "Stop the press!"

Miriam complied.

sixteen

"Gotta hand it to ya, Casey-girl," Bedie said the next day. "For a foreigner with no clue what you were doing, you sure have done us all proud."

Casey stared at the newspaper on the counter. "Wonder where they got that old picture," she muttered. Then she turned to Bedie. "I haven't done much. You're the one responsible for all the changes."

Bedie smacked her favorite steel spatula against the shiny red countertop. "Goes to show how little you know."

"I never claimed to know much of anything, if you'll remember."

"That's not what I meant, and you know it. Because you didn't know what all and how we'd been doing things for the last fifty years, you made changes left and right. And guess what?"

"What?"

"They were good ones." Bedie poured herself a mug of coffee and clambered up onto the stool next to Casey's. "It never woulda come to any one of our minds to turn this place into a buffet. But business sure's been great since you went ahead and did it. I bet you we're making twice what the Saylors did in a week."

"That's not such a big deal. Sooner or later someone would have thought of it."

In that uncanny way she had, Bedie changed her tone. "Sure, honey, but it wasn't some vague someone who did it. It was you. You thought of it, you put the idea together, took the risk to try it, and coddled it along until it became a hit.

That takes guts and vision, and you brought that with you when you came."

"I just didn't know any better than to rock the boat. I rocked it and am still stunned I didn't sink it like all the other boats I've rocked before."

Bedie dismissed her words with a wave. "Don't you think you ought to give the Lord more credit than that?"

"What do you mean?"

"Casey-girl, you've blessed and blessed and blessed this town since the moment you got here. It's about time you recognized His hand in all that's happened."

"You have it all wrong, Bedie. You're the one who's made it all happen. Your food's the best everyone who tastes it has ever had. And as far as who's blessed who—"

"Whom, girl. Don't you go forgetting that education I bet your daddy paid plenty for."

Casey winked. "*For which* my daddy paid plenty."

"Fine, fine." Bedie took a long swig of caffeine. "Doesn't go changing nothing that matters here. You've been a blessing to me and those kids."

"You're the ones who've blessed me. You're all such a joy. I can't tell you how much I love working with you."

Bedie's wrinkled and age-spotted hand patted hers. "You know what, Casey-girl? This is just how God goes around sharing His wealth. He puts folks in the path of others at just the right time and for just the right reason. That's why He brought you to us when He did."

"But—"

"No buts about it." Bedie's chin stuck out in the way Casey now knew meant that nothing and no one would budge her from her stance. "God's never wrong, and Rod's right this time. You're the best thing's hit Eden in a long time, and you're the best Citizen of the Month to start out with."

"You're nuts," Casey said, "but I love you, anyway."

"Aha! Toldja, didn't I? God's got your heart right where it belongs. Now all you gotta do is tell everyone you've come home for good."

"What?"

"Yep, Casey-girl, that's right. You better go tell the whole world you're not ever leaving Eden, Texas, much less that hunk Police Chief Rod Harmon. Ain't gonna find nothing like this town or that man in Dallas, and you know it. That's what God brought you here to learn."

For long moments, Casey couldn't draw breath. Then she shook her head. "I'm only here until my parents sell the diner, Bedie. You know that. And as for Rod. . ."

A sad little twinge crossed her heart. Nevertheless, she continued. "Rod's been wonderful, with all his help. But there's nothing between us. We're just friends."

Her conscience leaped up and waved wildly. *How about those kisses? And what about that trust deal? Friends, huh? Just friends? Yeah, right.*

Bedie said nothing, but her piercing eyes stared on. Which only made Casey protest further.

"I came to prove to my parents that I could do something right, and I've done it." She smiled. "I have, haven't I?"

Now if she could just convince her parents.

But that was another matter. "Bedie, you know how he hates Dallas and everything to do with it. I'm from Dallas."

"Piffle! Your mama just made the mistake of birthing you there. You're no more from Dallas than I am. You're an Edenite if ever there was one."

She wished. But Casey didn't dare give Bedie any more fuel.

"I'm just a temporary fix for the diner, which really should open right away if we want to make today's goal."

Bedie's look said Casey hadn't fooled her. But Casey had nothing more to say. Bedie's words had hit their mark.

As the day progressed, Casey could no longer avoid the truth. She was falling in love with Rod, just as she'd feared she might do. But that didn't mean they had a future together. He hadn't spoken of anything between them. The only thing she knew with any certainty was that he wanted nothing to do with Dallas.

Casey came from Dallas; her family still lived there.

She couldn't think a handful of kisses meant more than just that—simple kisses at an emotional time. She'd be crazy to put more weight on them than they merited. And she had noticed Rod's interest in and compassion for everyone he met.

Casey functioned on some weird kind of autopilot for the rest of the day. She greeted customers, asked the right questions, and made the right comments at the right time; she rang up bills and carried out the business of the diner.

Bedie's comments stayed in her mind. Had God brought her to Eden for a reason?

She'd never thought the Almighty would take interest in that kind of details, especially when there were so many other, more important things for Him to fix. There was world hunger to conquer; He could pick a war, any war to end; a cure hadn't yet been found for cancer—or the common cold, for that matter; there was even global warming to consider, whatever that really meant.

That the heavenly Father might care about her—insignificant, unimportant Calamity Casey—boggled the mind. Had He brought her to Eden for a purpose? Did the diner matter so much to Him?

Did Casey herself?

Where did Rod fit into all this?

The handsome police chief hadn't said a word about forever—not even a date for tomorrow night or any such thing, after all. So what would give Bedie the idea the man had love and wedding bells in mind?

She interrupted her ruminations to ring up another bill.

"Them Swedish meatballs were plumb fantabulistic, Casey Hunt."

"Thanks, Whit. That's just what we like to hear. Don't forget, now. Tomorrow's Country Cookin' Day."

He smacked his lips. "Can almost taste Bedie's pork chops, sour-cream mashed potatoes, and marinated cukes already."

Casey leaned forward. "Tell you what."

Whit stretched out his long neck.

She whispered. "If you come early, I'll sneak you an extra slice of her peach pie."

"With vanilla ice cream?"

"À la mode's the way you like it, and I don't forget."

The older gent clutched his chest. "Ah, Casey Hunt, ya stole my heart. Won't you marry me, darlin'?"

She fluttered her hand before her face. "Whoo—ee! If this is the way you courted Bedie, I can't figure out why she never said yes."

"Bah! That old hen's all set in her ways." Whit headed for the door. "What I need is a young chick like you."

His comment elicited cheers and whistles. Casey laughed with everyone else. In one way, Bedie was right. The diner, Eden as a whole, did feel like home. It had extended that elusive welcome Casey had longed for and hadn't found— until she came here.

But—and it was a big "but"—had she really accomplished what she'd set out to do? It seemed that she'd cleaned up more messes than accomplished anything of note. True, the diner was doing well, but then again, it had been doing well before she took over.

Had she had an impact, or had she just slipped into someone else's shoes?

Did she belong in Eden? For how long?

And what about Rod? How did he figure in her life?

Casey took a deep breath then dove right in.

"Lord?" she whispered, "what do You have in mind for me?"

❧

"Woo-hoo!" Paddy crowed. "Chief Rod's got a girl."

Rod took up his guitar and fought the blush with all he had. It didn't work. His ears burned hotter than ever.

"I doubt that's part of tonight's Bible study," he said. "Anyone know the verse?"

"Hebrews 1:6!" the boy announced—correctly.

"Fine, but what does it mean, with regard to the rest of the chapter, and especially when you considered the lesson?"

Paddy made a number of good points, but it wasn't until Molly chimed in that Rod really sat up and took notice.

"It means more than that, Paddy," the quiet girl said. "The verse refers to us all, but only when we open ourselves up to go where God wants to lead us. There've been times when I had the chance to perform, but because I let fear get the better of me, I didn't do it. Who knows what blessing I missed?"

Real pain filled the girl's words, as real as the pang that shot through Rod. But before he had a chance to look within, Sarah Anne spoke.

"I know what Molly means. I quit my job at the diner on account of the mess we made after the Saylors left. Now, with Miss Casey running the place, these guys"—she gestured at the diner's new staff—"are having fun and making enough money to open savings accounts. All because I got scared of what went wrong and what else might happen."

"I'm just glad Miss Casey came," Alyssa offered. "She's made that diner like a home for everyone. I just hope and pray she's found herself a home with us. It's the least we can do for her, to welcome her and make her feel she belongs. You know?"

Rod gave the kids a slow, measured nod.

Home. He knew what it meant, and he knew it better

than most. He'd come home from Dallas, certain that Eden was the place for him. Nothing had happened since then to change his mind. Now, however, Casey had crept into a private part of his heart, and he feared what might happen if he let her make a home there, just as she had in the diner and Eden as a whole.

Would she ask him to leave the town that meant so much to him and go back where she'd come from? Or would his heart demand to stay home and make him turn his back on her?

It made no sense to deny his growing feelings for the hippie wannabe turned successful restaurateur. He was falling in love with Casey Hunt. He just didn't know if that love would bring him the Lord's blessing, or if it would instead bring him grief.

He offered a silent prayer, and after his hushed "amen" he realized that a dozen teens were staring at him, fascinated wonder, or maybe rampant curiosity, on their youthful faces.

"What? Do I have chocolate ice cream on my face?" He always tried for humor to deflect embarrassment.

"Nah," said Ben, the latest object of Sarah Anne's teenaged affection. "You just look kinda cow-eyed. I think the girls are right. You've got the hots—"

"Watch it, Ben," Rod warned. "We've talked about appropriate comments. That one falls in the inappropriate category, and you know it."

"Fine," the boy groused. "What I meant to say was that the girls think you're nuts about Miss Casey. They all picked a day for the wedding and can't wait to see who's right."

"What is wrong with you guys?" Rod shook his head. "I hardly know the woman, and you're thinking wedding day?"

"It's not just us," Molly said. "Miss Bedie and Whit Tucker and Miss Deely started it. They're sure it won't be much after Labor Day."

"But it's already July. What's everyone thinking?"

At the electric keyboard, Alyssa struck a chord. The group hummed the notes to Lohengrin, and the bells above began to chime.

Clang, clang, bong! Bong, bong, ding! Clang, clang, bong!

Mayhem ensued.

The siren went off down by Turnham's Hardware, where the town's auxiliary fire department stored its one and only truck. From the far corner of the church overhead, Rod heard the stampede of the missions' board members, who up until then had been in a meeting.

Through the open window, he heard screams, shouts, and bellows. He turned to his charges. "Go! There's a fire somewhere. Hurry home, and if it's at your place, don't go in, whatever you do."

They ran upstairs. The kids scattered and, with only a quick glance, he made sure the building was vacant then hurried outside.

The street teemed with friends and neighbors; some wrung their hands in worry, others craned their necks to try to spot the blaze. When no red glare hinted at fire, he cupped his hands around his mouth and yelled.

"It's not the fire alarm. There doesn't seem to be a fire. Get in your cars and follow the evacuation plan. I'm not sure what's happened, but we can't afford to take a chance."

A tug at his shirtsleeve made him look down. "Do you need a ride, Deely?"

The old woman nodded. "D'you think it's them aliens they're always talking about on that science channel? If it is, I sure don't want to miss 'em."

"I doubt it. It's probably just some spill out on the freeway. Let's hurry to my car so we can get out of here before it's too late."

They tried the sidewalk, but the congestion created by the alarmed residents kept them almost in place. Cars revved their engines, horns honked, women yelled at kids, kids squealed at the excitement.

What could have happened?

A second pull on his sleeve made him turn around. Ted stood at his side, her eyes wide with fear, her lower lip trembling.

"I'm so sorry," she said. "I didn't mean to make such a mess."

"What do you mean? What mess did you make? And why aren't you home with your family? You have to leave town."

She lowered her head and a riot of black curls covered her face. "That's just it. No one needs to leave town. There's no emergency. I rang the bells."

"What!" he cried.

"Uh-oh," said Deely.

Ted gave a sob.

"Rod!" Casey called from across the street. "What's happened?"

The former hippie wannabe wore a yellow Garfield T-shirt and denim shorts. He smiled in spite of the peace he now had to restore.

"Less than I feared a moment ago, and much, much less than everyone else does."

"I don't get it. Where's everyone going?"

"Nowhere, if I can help it." He turned and ran back into the church. He took the steps to the steeple two by two, praying he was in time to avert even a simple fender bender.

He grabbed the rope to the main bell and yanked with all he had. *Clang, clang, clang, clang, clang. Clang, clang, clang, clang, clang.*

By the time he hit the third set of "all clear" chimes, the noise outside started to die down.

A quick swipe at his brow dried the sweat that dripped into his eyes. "Thank You, Jesus. I'm so glad I made it."

Then it occurred to him that he still had the worst job before him. What was he going to do about Ted?

He took the stairs down at a much slower pace than he'd run up. Each step brought him a greater measure of dread. What could have made the girl ring the bells? She had pulled crazy stunts from time to time, but since Casey put her to work at the diner, he thought they'd become a thing of the past.

"Father God," he pled, "help me deal with this girl. I've never had to do anything like this before, and I don't want to make a mistake."

He found Ted and Casey on the steps to the church, the woman's arm around the teen's shoulders. Their heads were close, and he could hear them, even though they spoke in murmurs. He came closer when what he really wanted was to walk away.

"It was just a joke," Ted said.

Casey nodded. "A practical joke."

"Yeah, real practical. I made everyone run for their lives."

"It backfired, all right. But I don't think anything too awful happened."

"That won't make a difference. Chief Rod was really mad when I told him I rang the bells."

Rod watched a pair of taillights turn the corner. Who could blame him?

"Did you tell him it was supposed to be a joke?"

"Do I look like I have a death wish?"

"What do you mean?"

"Chief Rod takes his job very, very seriously. And I just disturbed the peace—*big time*."

He'd never thought his devotion to his job would scare the kids. He'd have to talk to them about it. The last thing he wanted was to put up that kind of wall. He believed communication was the key when it came to teens.

"You know," Casey said, "I've been known to mess up here and there." Then she laughed. "Nah. Around home they call me Calamity Casey. I can't seem to get anything right."

"You?"

The disbelief in Ted's voice warmed Rod's heart. Casey needed to hear that.

"The very same." Casey sighed, and Rod wished he could comfort her.

She went on. "You know what I learned recently?"

"What's that?"

"That if you do mess up, you'll still live another day."

"I know that."

"Hang on," Casey said. "What I mean to say is that there's nothing you can't overcome. An apology goes a long way. Are you sorry you rang the bells?"

"I'm not sure I'm sorry I *rang* the bells, but I am sorry I scared everyone."

"Try a little harder, Ted. Is it okay for someone to run up to the belfry and ring the bells for fun?"

"Well, no, but—"

"Let me tell you a secret. There are no buts in this mess-up-recovery business. You face up to your mistakes, apologize, ask forgiveness, and do the best you can to make amends."

"What if I can't make amends? I mean, everyone got scared, they ran out, and then realized they had nothing to be scared of. How'm I going to make amends for that?"

"Try starting at the beginning," Casey suggested. She slipped a dark ringlet behind Ted's ear, and Rod saw the moisture on the girl's cheeks.

"Where's that?"

"Right where you and I started." Casey's patience surprised Rod. He'd never expected it. She added, "Now. Are you sorry you rang the bells?"

"In a way I guess I am—but I'm really, *really* sorry I scared everyone and upset Chief Rod and made a mess of everyone's evening."

"Then, kiddo, that's the beginning. Find Chief Rod and tell him how you feel. See where that takes you. Then you do the same for the whole town. A letter to Mrs. Nutley might do the trick—you know, for the newspaper."

"That's an idea."

"So we have a plan." Casey stood and held out her hand. Ted took it and rose to her mentor's side. "Let's go put it in motion, kiddo. You need to catch some sleep if you're going to carry heavy trays tomorrow."

"You mean you're not going to fire me?"

"No, Ted, I'm not going to fire you. I'm going to keep watching you do the great job you've done since the day I hired you."

The girl threw her arms around Casey's neck, her sobs of joy loud in the now quiet night.

"I love you, Miss Casey."

Rod saw Casey draw a sharp breath. A tear rolled down her cheek. "I love you, too, Ted. I love you, too."

And he loved Casey.

He couldn't let Calamity Casey leave town.

seventeen

An hour after Ted's stunt, Casey hung up the phone, her hands still shaky. What was she going to do now?

Mom had a buyer for the diner. And she was bringing him to see the place the next day.

What a day—evening, really. First they'd had to deal with Ted's escapade. Then Casey came home to her mother's message on the answering machine. What should she expect next? A plague of locusts? An invasion of frogs?

Her stomach twisted into knots.

She didn't want to leave Eden, but once the diner sold, what did she have to keep her here?

Her heart, for one. The town—and the chief of police—had stolen it away.

Then there was all the hard work she'd done at the diner. She'd put so much effort into the improvements that the place felt more than a little like her own. She didn't want someone to come in and rip up the stools she was about to install. She didn't want someone to take down her curtains. And she especially didn't want anyone to fire Bedie and the kids.

She sank into the cushy sofa, its plush toast-colored upholstery a meager comfort. She'd even fallen in love with the little apartment behind the diner.

The phone rang a while later, and, afraid it would be her mother again, she let the machine pick up. But it wasn't Mom. It was Rod.

"Hi," he said. "I wanted to tell how much I appreciate what you did for Ted tonight. I'm afraid I would have turned all cop on her and made a bigger mess of the situation. You're one terrific lady, Casey Hunt, and I'm glad you came to Eden."

At the beep that signaled the end of his call, her tears fell in earnest.

Even Goliath's fuzzy bulk failed to warm the icy feeling in her heart. For the first time in her life she'd done something really, really right. And somehow it still had turned out all wrong. She'd made a home for herself in Eden, but now she was going to have to leave.

She tried to pray, but the sobs got in her way. Time went by, she didn't know how much, and then someone knocked on the door.

Even though she didn't want to see anyone, she didn't want to be rude. Where else would she be at this time of night but here? Whoever had come to see her would think she'd turned them away without a care.

"Rod! Why are you. . .I mean, what are you doing here?"

"I called a couple of minutes ago and got worried when you didn't answer. It's kind of late for you to be out."

Evidently, she did a lousy job of hiding her tears, because he didn't take his gaze from her eyes. "I see I had reason to worry. What's wrong?"

She turned away. "Nothing, really. My mother called. She has a buyer for the diner, and I guess it caught me by surprise." She swallowed hard. "I realized how much I'm going to miss everyone."

He followed her, made her face him again, and curved a finger under her chin. "Casey, look at me. You don't have to leave. Nobody wants you to."

"But once the new owner arrives, there won't be any reason for me to stay."

"Maybe not at the diner," he said. "Look at me. Please."

He didn't let her do otherwise. What she saw in his blue

eyes took her breath away.

"Don't you think," he said, "that it's time to stop running from yourself? What is it you really want?"

She turned her back on him again. She wanted him, of course, and the diner and her life in Eden, too. But those weren't things she dared to say.

"Okay," he said. "Since you won't speak, I'll tell you what I want." He placed his hands on her shoulders. "I want you."

She gasped.

He squeezed. "Don't say anything—not yet. Just listen. I know we haven't known each other long, but I know I want to know you better. I think we could build a wonderful life together. But it won't happen if you don't let yourself accept what God's given you."

"Don't you see?" she cried. "I'm a mess. I can't even do the right thing the right way. Besides, what you need is a talented, competent woman. A chief of police deserves more than Calamity Casey at his side."

"Let me decide what I want, Casey. And right now, what I want is a chance with you."

She sobbed. "You're just being your usual kind, compassionate self. You see that I don't want to leave Eden, and so you want to try to make things right for me. But I can't let you sacrifice yourself like that. You need to find the right woman for you, the one that God really has waiting somewhere for you."

He ground his teeth. "So you're turning down my proposal."

"That wasn't a proposal."

"Then what was it?"

"I don't know, but I know it's not right." She went to the door. "You're the nicest man I know, Rod, but I need to be alone right now. My mother and the buyer will be here in the morning. I have to—to prepare."

He gave her a hard stare. "If that's the way you want it."

"It is."

At the door, he paused. "Good night, Casey Hunt."

As she locked up behind him, Casey couldn't help thinking his words sounded more like a final good-bye.

It should have made her feel better, but instead, it broke her heart in two.

❧

The next morning, armed with a thick folder of documents, she opened up the diner. The bank statements showed the marked increase in revenue since she'd reopened the place. And the cost of her small improvements wouldn't make much of a dent in the profit.

Success should feel a lot better than it did.

In the kitchen, she gathered her crew. She blinked to keep away the fresh tears. "I have news for you."

"We heard," Bedie said, her expression hard, her eyes angry. "I also heard you're on your way out of town. I expected more from you, Casey Hunt."

The kids didn't give an inch.

"I always said I'd stay until my parents found a buyer for the Saylors." Casey went to the cash register. "I'm sorry you thought otherwise."

Bedie snorted then muttered, "And she'd better see what's dangling before her nose and come to her senses right quick!"

At eleven fifteen, Mom's navy blue sedan pulled up in front of the diner. Casey's stomach churned, and her shivers began again. She didn't want to go through this day. She wanted to be anywhere but here. She couldn't stand the thought of leaving town.

Casey gave her mother a hug and shook hands with the client, Mr. David Chang.

"You look well, dear," Wendy Hunt whispered when Mr. Chang peeked into the kitchen. "I like the uniform. It's a good look on you, but you do have some dreadful dark circles under your eyes. Maybe you should see Dr. Zucker when you get home."

Casey nodded then shook her head. She didn't need a doctor. She needed. . .she had no idea what she needed to get out of this latest mess she'd made.

Without a word, she handed over the file. She took a seat next to her mother in the booth farthest from the door. Her misery grew with every page Mr. Chang examined.

Then Alyssa tripped right next to their booth. "Whoops!"

Vegetable soup rained down on Wendy Hunt and David Chang. Casey watched in horror as a chunk of carrot slid down the man's nose.

"I'm so sorry," Alyssa said before she scooted off to the kitchen.

Casey rushed over and grabbed a clean towel from behind the counter. "Here, Mr. Chang. Let me help you with that."

She took his jacket to the kitchen while he used the towel on his sticky hair. A quick swab with a sponge got out most of the broth.

"Alyssa!" she said, once satisfied with her efforts. "How could you leave a customer after you made a mess like that? The least you could do was offer him a towel."

The girl kept her back to Casey, but again said, "I'm sorry."

Casey noted one absence. "Where'd Bedie go?"

"She just left a minute ago," Paddy said. "Said she needed some. . .some stuff. She said she'd be right back."

"Just be careful in here. It's very important that Mr. Chang see what a great job you all can do."

On her way back to the booth, a suspicious whistle picked up steam—literally. Casey poked her head back in the kitchen and found what she feared.

As if on cue, Paddy yelled, "She's gonna blow!"

Steam gushed from the coffee machine and the whistle reached its piercing peak. Customers made for the door.

"What's going on here?" asked the clearly worried David Chang. "I thought this place was a model of efficiency."

"Nothing, sir," Casey replied. "Nothing's going on. We've just experienced a minor mishap. We'll take care of it right away."

As the words left her lips, a *whoosh* roared from the vicinity of the grill. An orange glow ensued.

Bedie walked in the front door. "What's burning? I declare! I can't leave you kids alone for even the shortest little minute or so. Can't you all just do your jobs and not trash everything up? I've never seen such a place for disasters."

She disappeared into the kitchen and Casey heard the fire extinguisher do its job.

"Burning?" Mr. Chang exclaimed, his voice shrill. "Disasters?"

Panic eclipsed Casey's sense of betrayal. "No, no. . ."

"What is the meaning of this, Casey Elizabeth Hunt?" her mother asked. "You assured me everything was in perfect order. Explain yourself."

Casey nodded. "It is—I mean, it was. We were doing great until you came in. I don't understand what's happened. But I'm sure it's nothing to worry about. We'll have everything under control in no time at all."

Right then, a white streak shot across the room and landed on Goliath. Casey was sure she'd left him back in the apartment. Her mother was allergic to dogs. How'd he get out?

But that wasn't the worst yet. The white streak gelled into a fuzzy white cat that latched on to Goliath's ratty ear. The thing snarled and yanked, clawed and hissed at the dog.

No sissy, Casey's canine fought back. *"Aaaarooooof!"*

With a powerful shake of the head, he rid himself of the cat, but in the doing lost a tuft of ear fur.

"Where did that cat come from?" Casey asked in horror.

"Cat?" Bedie asked from the kitchen doorway. "Oh, there's Blanche. My cat."

"Well, get her out of here, Bedie. Look at Goliath's ear."

"Him."

"Him? What do you mean, 'him'?"

Bedie shrugged. "Blanche is a him, not a her."

The room fell silent—except for the shrieking coffee machine and hissing feline.

Casey glared at the winningest cook in the county. "Let me get this straight, Obedience Ramsey. You have a cat, a male cat, named *Blanche*?"

"Yep."

"And that would be because. . . ?"

"No big deal, Casey-girl. When Weezie gave me the kitten, he was too young for—well, for us to make out what he was, you know, to be sure he was a he instead of a she. Since he had fluffy fur and was all white, I gave him my favorite name: Blanche."

Casey shook her head. *The Twilight Zone* had nothing on Eden, Texas.

With a great deal of patience, she asked, "Why didn't you rename him when you realized he was a he?"

"Well, because the vet weren't really sure it was a he—*just* a he—right away. For a while there, we thought I had me something real special. I figured I'd go on some late-night TV show and make a bundle with my boy/girl cat."

Bedie shook her head. "But it didn't turn out that way. Blanche is just a he. And it was too late to change his name, so he stayed Blanche."

The wrongly named creature must've really objected to the name, because after hearing it said that many times, he pounced up onto the counter next to Casey, from where he launched himself onto Goliath's back.

"*Wooooof!*"

...sssss!"

"Get the ark," Ted cried. "The faucet went again!"

And, just as it had before, the pressurized flow of water knocked Casey off her feet.

"Wendy," David Chang said as he ran to the door, "I don't know what kind of life your daughter leads, but this is anything but a successful restaurant. I want nothing to do with the place."

Casey cringed. Mom wasn't going to be happy. One look at her maternal parent told her she'd really run out of luck.

"Casey Elizabeth Hunt—"

"Mrs. Hunt?" Rod held out his hand.

Where'd he come from?

"It's a pleasure to meet you," he said then turned aside. "May I introduce Roger Adams, Eden's esteemed mayor?"

Wendy Hunt's gaze spit flames even though her lips spoke polite nothings.

"Oh, I'm so sorry," he added with a wink for Casey. "I forgot. I'm Rod Harmon. We spoke recently. I'm the chief of police who honored your daughter. I'm so glad you decided to take me up on my offer. Mayor Adams has a proposal for you."

"Ahem," said the tall, thin man. "It's come to my attention that the diner has more uses than one. I'd like to proffer a business deal whereby the town will buy the place from the Saylors. We'd like to turn it into a job-training facility for teens while it serves the county's residents. It'll enable us to put to good use the talents of a number of our retirees, who, as you can imagine, have so much to offer our youth."

Casey gaped. She looked from her mother, to the mayor, to Rod, then back to her mother.

In a blur, an agreement was reached. "We do have one stipulation," the mayor added.

Mom frowned. "And that would be?"

"That Miss Hunt stay on and manage the enterprise. She has a great business head on her shoulders, and she is wonderful with people. We don't know what we'd do without her."

Hope leaped in Casey's chest.

Her mother's look of shock nearly killed it.

Rod's arm around her kept it alive. "I told you to trust me, didn't I?"

She looked into his blue eyes. "Did you. . . ?"

"With the help of a few of my—our—friends."

"You mean the coffee machine and the fire—"

"Even the plumbing and the flying fur. We had to do something to keep you from making the biggest mistake of your life. I did a pretty good job orchestrating it all, wouldn't you say? I'm proud of our results."

A dazed Wendy Hunt called her daughter's name. "Are you sure this is what you want, dear?"

Casey never looked away from Rod. "I'm sure, Mom, more sure than I've ever been before."

"Except maybe of God's miracles," Bedie added. "And if you haven't been sure of them up to now, I bet today'll get you there and quick, Casey-girl."

Casey smiled at the older woman, who now held her combative white cat. From the corner of her eye, she saw her mother shake her head and open the diner's door.

"I'll call you later, Casey. I'm afraid I don't understand a thing."

"There's nothing to understand, Mom," Casey replied, her gaze on Rod once again. "I finally found what I'd been looking for. By the grace of God, I'm finally home."

The bells at the Church of the Rock began to chime.

Casey gasped.

Rod smiled and wrapped his arms around her. "It's okay. I told everyone I'd have Ted ring them if things worked out right."

Tears of joy filled her eyes. "They did, didn't they?"

"Just like I told ya they would, Casey-girl." Bedie went to the door. She leaned out and yelled, "He's got his arms around her now, so you can all come back in. She ain't going anywhere."

"I won't let you go, you know," Rod said, his lips a whisper away from hers. "So will you say yes?"

"Yes," she said. "Oh, yes, Rod. Yes, yes, yes."

He kissed her.

The bells pealed again.

A Letter To Our Readers

Dear Reader:

In order that we might better contribute to your reading enjoyment, we would appreciate your taking a few minutes to respond to the following questions. We welcome your comments and read each form and letter we receive. When completed, please return to the following:

Fiction Editor
Heartsong Presents
PO Box 719
Uhrichsville, Ohio 44683

1. Did you enjoy reading *Hunt for Home* by Ginny Aiken?
   ❑ Very much! I would like to see more books by this author!
   ❑ Moderately. I would have enjoyed it more if

   _____
   _____
   _____

2. Are you a member of **Heartsong Presents**? ❑ Yes ❑ No
   If no, where did you purchase this book? _____
   _____

3. How would you rate, on a scale from 1 (poor) to 5 (superior), the cover design? _____

4. On a scale from 1 (poor) to 10 (superior), please rate the following elements.

   ____ Heroine   ____ Plot
   ____ Hero   ____ Inspirational theme
   ____ Setting   ____ Secondary characters

These characters were special because?_____

_____

_____

6. How has this book inspired your life?_____

_____

_____

7. What settings would you like to see covered in future
   Heartsong Presents books?_____

_____

_____

8. What are some inspirational themes you would like to see
   treated in future books?_____

_____

_____

9. Would you be interested in reading other **Heartsong
   Presents** titles?   ❏ Yes   ❏ No

10. Please check your age range:
        ❏ Under 18   ❏ 18-24
        ❏ 25-34   ❏ 35-45
        ❏ 46-55   ❏ Over 55

Name_____

Occupation _____

Address _____

Hearts♥ng

Any 12
Heartsong
Presents titles
for only
$27.00*

CONTEMPORARY ROMANCE IS CHEAPER BY THE DOZEN!
Buy any assortment of twelve *Heartsong Presents* titles and save 25% off of the already discounted price of $2.97 each!

*plus $2.00 shipping and handling per order and sales tax where applicable.

HEARTSONG PRESENTS TITLES AVAILABLE NOW:

___HP338 *Somewhere a Rainbow*, Y. Lehman
___HP341 *It Only Takes a Spark*, P. K. Tracy
___HP342 *The Haven of Rest*, A. Boeshaar
___HP349 *Wild Tiger Wind*, G. Buck
___HP350 *Race for the Roses*, L. Snelling
___HP353 *Ice Castle*, J. Livingston
___HP354 *Finding Courtney*, B. L. Etchison
___HP361 *The Name Game*, M. G. Chapman
___HP377 *Come Home to My Heart*, J. A. Grote
___HP378 *The Landlord Takes a Bride*, K. Billerbeck
___HP390 *Love Abounds*, A. Bell
___HP394 *Equestrian Charm*, D. Mills
___HP401 *Castle in the Clouds*, A. Boeshaar
___HP402 *Secret Ballot*, Y. Lehman
___HP405 *The Wife Degree*, A. Ford
___HP406 *Almost Twins*, G. Sattler
___HP409 *A Living Soul*, H. Alexander
___HP410 *The Color of Love*, D. Mills
___HP413 *Remnant of Victory*, J. Odell
___HP414 *The Sea Beckons*, B. L. Etchison
___HP417 *From Russia with Love*, C. Coble
___HP418 *Yesteryear*, G. Brandt
___HP421 *Looking for a Miracle*, W. E. Brunstetter
___HP422 *Condo Mania*, M. G. Chapman
___HP425 *Mustering Courage*, L. A. Coleman
___HP426 *To the Extreme*, T. Davis
___HP429 *Love Ahoy*, C. Coble
___HP430 *Good Things Come*, J. A. Ryan
___HP433 *A Few Flowers*, G. Sattler
___HP434 *Family Circle*, J. L. Barton
___HP438 *Out in the Real World*, K. Paul
___HP441 *Cassidy's Charm*, D. Mills
___HP442 *Vision of Hope*, M. H. Flinkman
___HP445 *McMillian's Matchmakers*, G. Sattler
___HP449 *An Ostrich a Day*, N. J. Farrier
___HP450 *Love in Pursuit*, D. Mills
___HP454 *Grace in Action*, K. Billerbeck
___HP458 *The Candy Cane Calaboose*, J. Spaeth

___HP461 *Pride and Pumpernickel*, A. Ford
___HP462 *Secrets Within*, G. G. Martin
___HP465 *Talking for Two*, W. E. Brunstetter
___HP466 *Risa's Rainbow*, A. Boeshaar
___HP469 *Beacon of Truth*, P. Griffin
___HP470 *Carolina Pride*, T. Fowler
___HP473 *The Wedding's On*, G. Sattler
___HP474 *You Can't Buy Love*, K. Y'Barbo
___HP477 *Extreme Grace*, T. Davis
___HP478 *Plain and Fancy*, W. E. Brunstetter
___HP481 *Unexpected Delivery*, C. M. Hake
___HP482 *Hand Quilted with Love*, J. Livingston
___HP485 *Ring of Hope*, B. L. Etchison
___HP486 *The Hope Chest*, W. E. Brunstetter
___HP489 *Over Her Head*, G. G. Martin
___HP490 *A Class of Her Own*, J. Thompson
___HP493 *Her Home or Her Heart*, K. Elaine
___HP494 *Mended Wheels*, A. Bell & J. Sagal
___HP497 *Flames of Deceit*, R. Dow & A. Snaden
___HP498 *Charade*, P. Humphrey
___HP501 *The Thrill of the Hunt*, T. H. Murray
___HP502 *Whole in One*, A. Ford
___HP505 *Happily Ever After*, M. Panagiotopoulos
___HP506 *Cords of Love*, L. A. Coleman
___HP509 *His Christmas Angel*, G. Sattler
___HP510 *Past the Ps Please*, Y. Lehman
___HP513 *Licorice Kisses*, D. Mills
___HP514 *Roger's Return*, M. Davis
___HP517 *The Neighborly Thing to Do*, W. E. Brunstetter
___HP518 *For a Father's Love*, J. A. Grote
___HP521 *Be My Valentine*, J. Livingston
___HP522 *Angel's Roost*, J. Spaeth
___HP525 *Game of Pretend*, J. Odell
___HP526 *In Search of Love*, C. Lynxwiler
___HP529 *Major League Dad*, K. Y'Barbo
___HP530 *Joe's Diner*, G. Sattler
___HP533 *On a Clear Day*, Y. Lehman
___HP534 *Term of Love*, M. Pittman Crane

(If ordering from this page, please remember to include it with the order form.)

Presents

__HP537	Close Enough to Perfect, T. Fowler		__HP589	Changing Seasons, C. Reece and J. Reece-Demarco
__HP538	A Storybook Finish, L. Bliss		__HP590	Secret Admirer, G. Sattler
__HP541	The Summer Girl, A. Boeshaar		__HP593	Angel Incognito, J. Thompson
__HP542	Clowning Around, W. E. Brunstetter		__HP594	Out on a Limb, G. Gaymer Martin
__HP545	Love Is Patient, C. M. Hake		__HP597	Let My Heart Go, B. Huston
__HP546	Love Is Kind, J. Livingston		__HP598	More Than Friends, T. H. Murray
__HP549	Patchwork and Politics, C. Lynxwiler		__HP601	Timing is Everything, T. V. Bateman
__HP550	Woodhaven Acres, B. Etchison		__HP602	Dandelion Bride, J. Livingston
__HP553	Bay Island, B. Loughner		__HP605	Picture Imperfect, N. J. Farrier
__HP554	A Donut a Day, G. Sattler		__HP606	Mary's Choice, Kay Cornelius
__HP557	If You Please, T. Davis		__HP609	Through the Fire, C. Lynxwiler
__HP558	A Fairy Tale Romance, M. Panagiotopoulos		__HP610	Going Home, W. E. Brunstetter
__HP561	Ton's Vow, K. Cornelius		__HP613	Chorus of One, J. Thompson
__HP562	Family Ties, J. L. Barton		__HP614	Forever in My Heart, L. Ford
__HP565	An Unbreakable Hope, K. Billerbeck		__HP617	Run Fast, My Love, P. Griffin
__HP566	The Baby Quilt, J. Livingston		__HP618	One Last Christmas, J. Livingston
__HP569	Ageless Love, L. Bliss		__HP621	Forever Friends, T. H. Murray
__HP570	Beguiling Masquerade, C. G. Page		__HP622	Time Will Tell, L. Bliss
__HP573	In a Land Far Far Away, M. Panagiotopoulos		__HP625	Love's Image, D. Mayne
			__HP626	Down From the Cross, J. Livingston
__HP574	Lambert's Pride, L. A. Coleman and R. Hauck		__HP629	Look to the Heart, T. Fowler
			__HP630	The Flat Marriage Fix, K. Hayse
__HP577	Anita's Fortune, K. Cornelius		__HP633	Longing for Home, C. Lynxwiler
__HP578	The Birthday Wish, J. Livingston		__HP634	The Child Is Mine, M. Colvin
__HP581	Love Online, K. Billerbeck		__HP637	Mother's Day, J. Livingston
__HP582	The Long Ride Home, A. Boeshaar		__HP638	Real Treasure, T. Davis
__HP585	Compassion's Charm, D. Mills		__HP641	The Pastor's Assignment, K. O'Brien
__HP586	A Single Rose, P. Griffin		__HP642	What's Cooking, S. Sattler

Great Inspirational Romance at a Great Price!

Heartsong Presents books are inspirational romances in contemporary and historical settings, designed to give you an enjoyable, spirit-lifting reading experience. You can choose wonderfully written titles from some of today's best authors like Hannah Alexander, Andrea Boeshaar, Yvonne Lehman, Tracie Peterson, and many others.

When ordering quantities less than twelve, above titles are $2.97 each.
Not all titles may be available at time of order.

SEND TO: **Heartsong Presents** Reader's Service
P.O. Box 721, Uhrichsville, Ohio 44683

Please send me the items checked above. I am enclosing $ _____
(please add $2.00 to cover postage per order. OH add 7% tax. NJ
add 6%). Send check or money order, no cash or C.O.D.s, please.
To place a credit card order, call 1-800-847-8270.

NAME _____

ADDRESS _____

CITY/STATE _____ ZIP_____

HPS 6-05

HEARTSONG

PRESENTS

If you love Christian romance...

You'll love Heartsong Presents' inspiring and faith-filled romances by today's very best Christian authors...DiAnn Mills, Wanda E. Brunstetter, and Yvonne Lehman, to mention a few!

When you join Heartsong Presents, you'll enjoy 4 brand-new mass market, 176-page books—two contemporary and two historical—that will build you up in your faith when you discover God's role in every relationship you read about!

Imagine...four new romances every four weeks—with men and women like you who long to meet the one God has chosen as the love of their lives...all for the low price of $10.99 postpaid.

To join, simply visit www.heartsong presents.com or complete the coupon below and mail it to the address provided.

$10.99

Mass Market 176 Pages

- -

YES! Sign me up for Heartsong!